A Book Of Practical Monsters

Little Book of Pain #3

Craig Brownlie

Working with characters such as these, I stand on the shoulders of giants and dream of seeing half as far as they have.

***

Contents © 2024 Craig Brownlie

Cover & Internal art © 2024 Douglas Draper

CONTENTS

1. Thanksgiving Dinner Is At Igor's This Year — 1

2. Fancies Curled Around Images — 18

3. Gil Returns A Favor — 36

4. We Did Little Good To Each Other — 55

5. This New Year's, Gil Will Entertain Alternative Opinions, Brian Will Wear A Suit, And Lionel Will Meet A Nice Girl — 85

6. Most of the Evil — 101

7. I Measure My Life Out With Coffee Spoons — 116

8. Disturbing The Dust — 136

9. About A Zombie — 153

Also by Koj Books — 169

About the author — 170

Thanksgiving Dinner Is At Igor's This Year

The Monster dragged his heavy feet up to the counter and placed his passport before the INS officer. "Morning," he said with a voice which sounded fresh from the grave, resonated across a bone xylophone, and vibrated through a henge of granite.

The officer held the photo up for comparison, "Is this you?"

"I've had a little work done since it was taken."

"I see you have dual citizenship. You've been in Canada for a while. I hope you haven't overstayed your welcome." The officer sounded cheerful about it. Pembina, North Dakota, tended to be slow at 3 a.m. on a Tuesday.

"The people of Belcher have been very welcoming. I don't always run into kindness."

"Purpose of your trip?" The officer dropped the passport.

"I'm joining friends for holiday dinner."

"Labor Day cookout, ehh?" smiled the officer.

"Thanksgiving."

"You're a little early." The officer retrieved the passport and compared it to the paperwork. "It shouldn't take so long to reach anywhere in the lower forty-eight."

"You'd be surprised what I run into."

The officer grinned. "Sterling t. Gray is your legal name? Lower case t? What does it stand for?"

"The person who made the passport for me said it stood for 'the.'"

"I'm afraid you're going to meet my supervisor," said the officer.

"This is what I meant."

***

Brian the Zombie sat on the tombstone and rested a withered forearm on a statue of a Pomeranian named Spinner. Brian liked dogs but hadn't come across any he could pet since the Great Mall Slaughter when he lost all sense of himself.

Grateful to have found structure for his existence, the Zombie shambled around the continental United States with the seasons, always planning to be somewhere special for the holidays. Halloween through Valentine's Day he felt a little human again- this year especially so, ever since he received Igor's invitation.

***

The Creature climbed into the houseboat and sat at his work desk. Some idiot had rebranded his favorite social media platform. He had one instant message: "Gil, are you coming to [turkey icon] Day dinner? I want to lay in the necessaries if so."

The Creature used an oversized keyboard which he had special-ordered. He typed, "It's not my holiday." He ranted online about how the government covered up its research into cryptids while waiting for a reply.

"We all have things to be thankful for, including one another."

The Creature considered the array of available icons and sent a thumbs up.

***

The accountant woke in a cornfield and caught sight of a beautiful sunrise. Yesterday Lionel had sent his last actuarial calculations to the members of his makeshift family before the holiday season kicked into gear. Unfortunately, he had also waited until the last minute to do the lunar calendar, only to realize a blue moon would be due in late November.

For now, he needed underwear and a flea dip.

***

The Mummy appreciated ordering ahead. Awkwardly navigating her mobile home into the drive-through, she wanted to grab the coffee and go. The cashier stared after her as the RV pulled away.

The department store across the street offered a huge parking lot. Still, Farrah located the hearse easily. Mira had parked away from the lights near the sewer which ran at the far end. Waiting, Farrah listened to Afropop Worldwide on the radio.

Her phone dinged even as the hearse rustled.

A drumstick hand knocked at the back door and in stepped Mira, looking perky and grumpy. The vampire held out a hand, "Coffee."

"My amulets aren't selling on the dark web like they used to," said Farrah. "Remind me why I buy you a beverage to waste."

"The scent remains a powerful stimulant." Mira removed the lid from her cup and inhaled. "Online auctions are dying. You should invest in high end jewelry." She dabbed a little coffee below her ears. "Do you do all your decorating with pyramids?" Mira eyed a stone model on the table. "I see everyone finally responded in the affirmative to the invitation."

***

Stomping down the stairs, Igor hummed tunelessly. He sharpened his carving knife as he went. The cacophony set the meat in the basement into riots of protest.

As opposed to most in-home dens of iniquity, Igor kept his processing space pristine and well-lit. He had cleared away all the junk accumulated by the previous owner. Out went the casement windows and the unsanitary walls and floors. Igor did all the work himself. Prior experience in numerous laboratories over the centuries had taught him how handy a person could be with a little tenacity and a fearless approach to self-injury.

Reminding himself to be humane always, Igor smiled at his victims. Igor had learned from his résumé of mad scientists that he should never lose touch with his inner kindness. He gently placed the knife on the metal table. Approaching softly, Igor clicked his tongue soothingly.

The middle-aged man inside the cage tried to scream.

"Now, now," said Igor. "We can both agree I'm no Doctor Frankenstein. I learned my surgery at the side of the great vivisectionists, but these fingers don't always work as well as either of us would hope." He held his hands out, displaying swollen bursa, a backwards trio of knuckles, and a hideous scar along one palm. "I did warn you about screaming, didn't I?"

Igor reached through the bars and pinched the man's belly. Turning to the next cage, he smiled benignly at the woman inside. "Have you ever heard of turducken? They put a chicken inside a duck inside a turkey and cook it all up. I find it quite inspirational, don't you?"

The woman gestured furiously, causing her shackles to clatter.

Igor nodded, "I agree this is quite the predicament."

Patting her knee, Igor continued, "Let's face it, neither of you had anywhere in particular to be today unless I insisted you participate in our feast. You, dear, have spent the last dozen major holidays behind drawn shades, masturbating to the Hallmark channel until your carpal tunnel acted up." He turned to the terrified man, "But I can't ignore you either. Not a single piece of mail to anyone other than 'Occupant' since the Bush administration. I know! It's true whichever administration I mean.

"But let me assure you that I've had the numbers run. I have this dear friend, Lionel, and he is an actuarial accountant. He's going to be here for dinner later today. In fact, my makeshift family is coming over. I hope we can take turns hosting going forward. This is the inaugural event. Frankly I don't enjoy the drafty castles or the campgrounds. Give me a nice suburban McMansion like my dear old home and I am as happy as the Creature from the lagoon in his... well... lagoon."

Crossing to his key rack, Igor kept talking, "Of course, we did the research ahead of time on proposed victims. We have to gather the data. Lionel loves his statistics.

"He should have become a doctor like the pack desired but I am glad he found a calling." Igor returned to the cages and smiled broadly. "I can absolutely assure you that neither of you has any sort of interesting future ahead of you, certainly not beyond Thanksgiving dinner.

"I'm so sorry. I try not to misplace my manners. Happy Thanksgiving!"

***

The doorbell rang and Igor called out for help answering it. Then he turned from the stove. "I may need to have my head examined, forgetting no one has arrived yet."

Opening the front door, Igor found a shivering half-dressed man.

"Lionel! You're early," Igor stepped aside so his guest could dash inside. "I went to bed early last night since one has to start the preparations before sunrise. Did we have a full moon?"

Lionel nodded vigorously.

"Found yourself at loose ends out in the woods? Personally, I would have prioritized pants over shirts, but you do you. Nice, durable fanny pack though," Igor pointed with a ladle at the staircase to the second floor. "You may find attire in the closet in the first bedroom on your right. Not the left."

As Igor returned to the kitchen, he heard a yell from above. "I said the right!" Then muttering to himself, "And this is why my laboratory is boobytrapped. They never listen. Curiosity kills werewolves more often than silver. "

Looking sheepish, Lionel joined his host in the kitchen after a suitable interval for his ablutions. "I had no expectation of you owning anything remotely in my size."

Raising a deboning knife in one hand and viscera in the other, Igor considered his own width, height, and depth. He nodded. "My foresight has long been appreciated."

"So, you knew about the full moon?"

"I prepare for most eventualities," Igor smiled, his huge teeth a row of tombstones. "Your average mad scientist is not a planner, more a dreamer. You must appreciate the importance of planning in your life?"

Lionel grabbed a carrot and nibbled the tip. "You mean as an actuary? It's odds really, which is more like soothsaying." He tossed the carrot in the corner and selected a bone from the plate beside Igor. Cracking it, Lionel sucked out marrow. "Always good to be the first on the scene if you want the choice bits." He slurped thoughtfully before asking, "Do you suppose Gil will be joining us?"

***

Farrah and Lionel sat in the living room watching the football game when the doorbell rang. Wearing a bloodstained "Kiss the cook" apron, Igor bustled through to the door, "Please don't stand up."

A yard away, Igor pulled up hard in his tracks and covered his nose, even as Farrah and Lionel frowned at a stench.

Igor studied his options and settled on, "Gil?" he called. "Listen, there's an outdoor shower around back for the summer time. The water should still be on! Sometimes I find it easier for washing away stains! I'll pass out Clorox and body spray!"

Turning to the duo engrossed in the game, Igor placed his hands on his hips, "More nuts?"

"Are they Brazilian?" asked Farrah.

"You have a little mess here," said Igor, dabbing at his own cheek.

Farrah reached up and pulled away a bandage, revealing a beetle. She screeched and covered it with her hand.

"You'll find what you need to repair your tear in the bathroom upstairs. Don't go in my laboratory."

Once Gil bathed, the trio welcomed him with open arms. Gil paused before the large portrait on the wall. "You don't look any different, Farrah."

"Who painted it again? They really captured my grandfather," said Lionel.

"I thought that Lionel was your great-grandfather. He was nothing like his father," said Farrah.

"Hogarth Putterdam. He's in all the museums now," said Igor before stepping out of the room.

"Gil, you should be in the painting," said Farrah.

Gil did not respond, so Lionel said, "I have a picture of you with Igor and my father." Under his breath, he added, "I know my own grandfather."

Igor brought out a tray, "For my first arrivals, special canapes, roasted garlic eyeballs. The recipe appeared in my inbox and I've been saving it for this occasion. Just imagine? They suggested sheep. I only had four on hand, so one for each of us."

Gil held up a clawed hand, "I'm pescatarian."

Farrah's eyeball squirted on her bandages, prompting Igor to offer a towel he carried for such an eventuality.

"I don't understand," said Lionel. "You eat fish eyeballs, right? What difference does it make where they're sourced? These are delicious, even better than raw. You should try a bite."

Gil crossed his arms. "I'll know where they came from."

"I have just the thing for you," Igor motioned them across the room to a new closet. "Ta-da!" He opened the doors to reveal a huge aquarium. "If you feel at all peckish anytime..."

Farrah pivoted toward the door. "Who else are we expecting?"

Gil answered, "Mira won't arrive until after dark. We're both staying at the Sunset Motel at the highway exit by the reservoir. We spoke last night before she went off to talk with a fisherman pulling his boat out of the water."

"Brian and Sterling could be here anytime," said Igor.

Farrah nodded, "One of them has arrived."

Lionel sniffed the air, "It's Brian." Then he thought of something, "Do we have to wait for Mira to start dinner? Fine, then I'm eating a second eyeball."

***

Mira arrived a half hour after the sun dropped out of sight and apologized for oversleeping.

Igor refused to serve the main course until everyone had taken their seat. This apparently included Sterling, who remained absent and had not even bothered to call.

The phone rang. Mira said what they all thought, "You still have a land line?"

"I'm such a homebody," responded Igor as he lurched out to the kitchen and answered.

Back at the table, everyone eavesdropped on the escalating tone of Igor's distress. After slamming down the handset, their host stomped into the dining room, creating new squeaks in the floorboards. "We need to go and bail Sterling out," he said through clenched teeth which came nowhere near aligning.

Farrah had driven her mobile home, so they piled in and spread out a little.

"You really like pyramids," commented Gil after bumping his head on a thematic mobile.

"They remind me of happier times," said Farrah as she backed out of Igor's driveway extra roughly causing Gil to take another thwack on the forehead.

"Come on! You're not going to tell me things were better in ancient times than now. We have sanitation and medicine," argued Lionel.

"I miss my family and my people! They worshipped me!" said Farrah.

"Like they had a choice," said Gil.

Mira placed a hand on Gil's forearm. "She's going through something." She raised a perfectly plucked eyebrow, "The bandaged one has a point. We are each unique in our own way, which can lead to a great loneliness."

"That's why I reached out," said Igor. "Sterling lives a nomadic life, but he might need to be reminded family is what you make it. I stood tableside when he came alive, but even a godfather can disappear from your life if you let him."

"And he had my number," admitted Mira, waving her mobile, "and I have a very impressive contact list if I say so myself."

"I get along fine alone on my boat," pouted Gil.

"You're here aren't you?" grimaced Brian.

At the Public Safety Building downtown, Farrah circled the block until she found an alley which satisfied their various needs for seclusion.

Igor stood, "All right, who's going in?"

"Lionel is the professional," suggested Gil.

"You're the most imposing," countered Lionel. "And Mira has a way with people."

"It is true," agreed Mira. "Igor is the host. This is his town. They must be aware of him."

"Not even a little bit," said Igor. He sat back down.

Farrah took his place in the middle of the cabin. "We all go," she insisted.

The Mummy led them out, but lagged behind by the time they reached the entryway. Late on a holiday, the signs in the atrium directed them to police intake down a hallway.

The desk sergeant watched the gang file into his tiny waiting area. "Halloween was last month."

Mira stepped forward, "Ah ha, humor. We are here to gather our friend to our bosom and take him to the feast table."

The officer looked to the others and gestured with his pen, silently asking if Mira could be for real.

Brian stepped forward.

"Nope, not happening," said the Sergeant. "I can't have such a stink lingering all night. You and you," he pointed at Farrah, "should go wait outside, not in the atrium, but air with a breeze. Maybe go stand by the smokers' spot."

Farrah took Brian by the hand and guided him out.

"Seriously, sir," Lionel approached the counter, "we would like to bail out Sterling... umm..." He looked to his companions.

"Green?" suggested Gil.

"It is a color," said Mira.

"Gray," Igor approached. "Sterling t. Gray is our friend's name. It's the turkey and the football and the beer making it so difficult to remember names... shall I go on?"

"Please don't," responded the officer. "Fill this out. We take most major credit cards."

They all looked at Lionel.

"Sure, the accountant carries his wallet." Lionel rooted around in his fanny pack.

"You buy it online? It looks like it's really well made," the policeman admired the wolfman's carryall.

Lionel scribbled and asked, "So, exactly what did he do? This form isn't too clear."

"He broke an Uber," the Sergeant smiled. "The driver says he broke the suspension and the two of them started arguing, whereupon your friend tore a door off the hinges. The responding officer picked the guy with that kind of strength to arrest." He reviewed the completed form. "I'll be right back."

"Who else is shocked that Sterling knew about Uber?" asked Gil.

Sterling appeared followed by the policeman. "He's all yours, though don't expect a tow truck to come out tonight if he breaks your car."

Sterling looked so embarrassed his knobs glowed red. "I apologize. This is what happens when I hurry to be on time."

***

"Shall we go around the table and say what we are thankful for?" suggested Igor.

"I'm too hungry," complained everyone.

"After the first helping," said Gil, carrying his plate to the aquarium in the other room.

Igor grinned, "Then I will bring out the roast."

Questions raced around the seating as they all wondered about the main course.

"Surely it is not turkey."

Igor's arms stretched wide to bear the platter. The human body appeared well-dressed and beautifully cooked. "Surely you have all heard of turducken?"

"Humans experiment needlessly," commented Mira. "They bore very easily, I believe."

"I call this her-bits'n'blood," Igor lowered the platter to the center of the table as Brian and Farrah scrambled to move the flowers and candles. Igor raised a carving set, "I'll take first honors and serve everyone. First pieces go to Lionel and Sterling. Neither of you eats people regularly, but special occasions and all."

"I've dabbled," confessed Lionel.

"You dare not conceive of my diet in the Arctic," added Sterling.

"I found a video that showed how to extract the esophagus and so many other bits came out. Once I pulled out the rest of the guts I had room for two special treats I used for stuffing," said Igor, inserting a hand into the newly exposed chest cavity. He had grabbed Brian's plate and slid two handfuls of warm brains out. "I considered jellying them, but a little spice and a nice long roast did wonders."

Next, Igor trimmed crispy skin and fat off for Farrah. "I honestly did not know what you might like best. Tell me for next year."

Farrah accepted the offering and immediately gobbled down a strip like bacon.

"I haven't forgotten you, Mira." Igor shoved a hand through the middle of the torso weakened by previous trimming and withdrew two pints of blood in cooking baggies. "Think pudding. I even have a long handled spoon for you."

Mira nodded, "You are truly sublime as a host and as a chef."

Igor served himself, "Now eat before it reaches room temperature."

***

Gil undid his pants. The sound of stitches stretching emanated from Sterling. Mira looked like a sated junkie. Lionel's belly had swollen so it jiggled against the table. Farrah loosened her bandages. Brian held the floor, apparently brightening with every bite of brains.

During a lull in the monologue, Igor turned to Mira and inquired, "Pumpkin or apple?"

"How droll," answered the vampire.

"Isn't there supposed to be a chemical in flesh which makes you tired?" wondered Lionel. "It's why everybody watches *Chitty Chitty Bang Bang* after Thanksgiving dinner."

"You're thinking of turkey," said Gil.

Brian spoke through suddenly half-lidded eyes, "It must be in brains."

"I'll have pumpkin," said Farrah, rising from the table. "Let me help with the dishes." Walking beside Igor, she leaned in and said, "Egyptians invented pie when I lived on the lower Nile."

Gil looked at Mira, "She is one princess who is willing to dirty her hands."

"Tell me, Gil, is your blood especially salty?" Mira tilted toward him, holding his gaze. "I would love to taste it."

Sterling waved a hand between them, "Actually, Farrah is a former pharaoh. She may have been a princess beforehand, but she likely dirtied her hands quite a bit overseeing her country."

Brain licked the last brain goo from his plate, "Are there any hand wipes?"

***

Everyone bunched at the door, offering hugs. Brian enveloped Farrah, but he pulled away trailing a strip of papyrus. Igor produced scissors and masking tape, though the story grew with each telling in coming years. Sterling and Brian agreed to walk for a few miles together, turning down Farrah's offer of a ride. Lionel helped Mira with her coat.

The vampire held up her hands, "Igor, this has been a sheer delight. I hope you can all join me in my humble abode for Christmas."

"It's the same castle, right?" said Gil.

"I moved it again after a conversation with a South African billionaire about avoiding income tax. You will each have a room to yourself." Mira opened the door. "We do presents after midnight mass on Christmas Eve." She transformed into a bat and flew outside.

"Naturally," said Sterling.

"Everyone will be there?" asked Igor.

Filled with gratitude, each guest departed with a nod, a shuffle, a scramble, a dash, or an amble.

FANCIES CURLED AROUND IMAGES

In Mira's nightmare, many faces appeared when the intruders raised the lid of her resting place. Many hands scrabbled around the edges, found purchase, and wrenched it away. The torchlight blinded her.

When the lid was actually yanked open, ripping her from those nightmares, she recognized the solitary face with its condescending expression. The stake barely missed her heart.

***

Sterling felt more uncomfortable than he had while living in his hut on the outskirts of a farm in Switzerland. Decades had passed, Sterling had experienced many extremes since, but this chair might as well be a torture device.

Sterling struggled to stir his tea and balance the fine china cup in his huge hands. "He was a great man."

"You missed a spectacular funeral," said Mira, seated in a matching chair and drinking thicker fluid from a matching teacup. "You need not have come. I'm sure you made a difficult journey on foot."

"I came as soon as I heard of Vlad's passing."

"He would be grateful," offered Mira. Her fangs showed as she sipped. "Honestly we could find other furniture."

"I was not made for narrow seats," admitted the Simulacrum. "Even though the local people did this to Vlad, you remain here?"

"You appreciate the importance of obscurity," answered the Vampire, "so needs must."

"Once I needed to live at the ends of the earth. I have since learned of many ways to hide, even in a crowd." Sterling stared into his drink even as he asked, "Did Vlad ever grow kinder toward you?"

Mira ignored the question. "To tell the truth, I have considered relocating. It would be a massive undertaking. I see the question already forming on your gray lips. Unlike you who has told of floating on an iceberg with nothing more than the clothes on his back, I would prefer to take this castle with me."

"Impossible!" said Sterling, even as his echo agreed.

Mira sipped the viscous contents of her cup and studied the Monster, as if deciding how much to trust a friend of her deceased husband. Then, she snapped her fingers, which sounded like the retort of two hollow sticks in a quiet forest.

A dumpy retainer entered the sitting room and stopped, his attention focused on the guest rather than his mistress.

Mira's eyes shifted between the two. "You share past familiarity?" As their silence grew heavy, she added, "Igor, out with it!"

Before another word entered the room, Sterling leapt at Igor and raised him high.

"Stop!" shouted Mira. "Explain yourselves!"

"This fiend tormented me when I stood chained and helpless!" bellowed Sterling.

"Put him down! If he merits punishment then it is mine to administer." She waited until a calmer air returned to the room. "This is the genius who will oversee my relocation. For now, Igor, affirm how you are acquainted with Sterling."

"I assisted a previous employer in animating the assembled parts," Igor dared a brief glower.

Sterling rose again to his feet and clenched his hands.

Nonplussed, Igor added. "As with any child, he required training and the scientist placed me in charge of Sterling's education."

"You waved fire in my face!" declared Sterling.

Igor walked up to the towering Monster, "How do you suggest I should have disciplined you?"

"You did worse!" emphasized Sterling.

"You're here aren't you? Drinking from fancy cups and sitting in a room surrounded by tapestries?" Igor ran a finger down the nearest wall hanging and raised a cloud of dust. "Could use a bit of cleaning, though."

"Consider what Vlad would do if he heard you insult my caretaking," Mira judiciously set her goblet down and leaned forward. "However, Vlad never employed enough help."

She motioned Igor closer. He resisted but neared the vampire.

"Why do I believe I own you?" Mira steepled her fingers and searched Igor's countenance. "Do not fear me, crooked little homunculus."

"He's the assemblage," managed Igor, pointing an accusatory digit across the room.

"Might I beg a boon?" asked Sterling. "Give me the finger extended in my direction."

"Rhymes with mucilage," added Igor, with a fearful glance at the contents of Mira's cup.

"Enough!" shouted Mira. "While I respect your ability to resist me-" she leaned back and clarified, "both of you manage it. Igor, you will continue to oversee the deconstruction and reconstruction of my glorious pile of stones. I want every arch and cellar, tower and secret passage disassembled and recreated."

Igor bowed and backed away.

Before he made his third step, Mira said, "But you could learn discipline. I want you to spend the day working in the stables with the boys."

Igor shook his head vigorously.

Mira called for an escort to take Igor away. Amid such hullabaloo, she noticed a smile spread across Sterling's face.

After an interlude of silence, Sterling said, "You appear to have recovered from any injuries suffered in the attack. Or in the months leading up to it."

Mira spoke into her drink, barely audible, "Vlad fought demons. He chose to do so alone."

"What would you have of me?" asked the Monster.

"I would have you keep me company while we wait."

Sterling sat still for an interminable length before he started tapping the arm of his chair. The index and middle fingers of his right hand danced across his legs. He blew bubbles in his tea and then sipped them in order to tickle his mouth. Boredom palpably weighed upon his shoulders. "For what do we sit in expectation?"

"Would you like a book?" asked Mira. She extracted the pocket watch previously in the possession of her deceased husband and checked the time. "I don't imagine I can watch you fidget for another ten minutes."

Sterling rose to bid farewell.

"Sit!" demanded Mira.

Sterling frowned with feeling before resettling himself. "I'll take the wider chair now, if you please."

Houseboys rearranged matters to the Monster's comfort. The next half hour passed as time does in a stagnant room with stoic acquaintances.

An elderly retainer eventually entered and spoke softly in Mira's ear. She made rapid hand signals. Mira smiled at Sterling, raising goose pimples on his forearms and wonder in his mind that he could experience such a sensation.

"A delivery has arrived from the village," announced Mira.

"And what do your villagers bring which your castle does not offer?" inquired the Simulacrum.

"Parcels destined for us do not always originate locally. Many come from distant lands, ordered by my beloved Vladimir when he still sucked the marrow from life. This is the reason I asked you to wait with me. You claim a long life, as do I... as did my departed lover, but now we shall gaze into the eyes of a being who dwarfs our claim."

***

"To your feet, old man!" ordered the Stable Master. He shook a rake in Igor's face.

"I've been threatened by geniuses, you wretched pittance," responded the ragtag man crumpled in a corner.

The Master lowered his implement and leaned against it. "So it may be, but I never studied threatening. You know why not?"

Igor shook his head.

"Because it doesn't matter what I say as long as I'm backed by the likes of the Count and Countess." The Master extended a helping hand, "What say you give me and the lads a wee bit of help with the load which just now arrived by cart from the village? It's guaranteed to be better than continuing to sit in our wee corner."

The cart sat by the lower entrance to the castle. It bore a large, long box which looked like a heavy burden to carry through the kitchen and up to where Mira waited. Igor preferred to supervise, but he no longer bore such power.

The cart driver stood atop the bed and tugged the covering cloth off the box, revealing a distinct coffin shape. The stable hands stopped. They refused to approach even as their master prodded their backs.

Igor stepped around the line of frightened youths. "It appears Egyptian, if I'm not mistaken," he said, inserting calmness alongside his exceptionally moist phrasing. "A gift for her highness, perhaps?" He raised an inquiring eyebrow at the driver.

"Whatever you want it to be, I always say," agreed the cart man. "The sooner it's off the sooner I'm paid and the sooner I'm at the tavern. They've announced a new entertainment for the evening. They're doing a contest where they ask questions and those who give the most answers win prizes. It's my understanding that the prizes are ale. Also, there's liable to be a whole set of questions about carts."

Igor leaned on one wheel of the vehicle, "You interest me strangely." He shook himself back to the present. "Come along, lads. I vouchsafe the box covered in disturbing images."

They made it all the way to the anteroom of the sitting room before one of the stable hands asked, "What do you suppose is inside such as this?"

"Fruit or veg," piped up one of the others, "it's always fruit or veg even when your mum promises a pudding."

Igor held up a hand for silence. "It's a dead body." He quickly returned his hand to the suddenly unsteady burden. As one, the pallbearers shifted left, then right and dashed forward into the sitting room.

Mira and Sterling sat terribly still, only their following eyes betrayed any alarm.

The ancient sarcophagus moved free of its bearers and slid several feet before coming to rest shy of the fireplace.

The servants held precariously still. The air in the room grew ever so slightly cooler as if filled with suppressed dismay.

"Mr. Furlong!" cried Mira.

Furlong the Stable Master stepped forward.

"Do you happen to have a tool for prying open the coffin?" asked Mira.

A desperate, mad smile appeared on Furlong's face, "I do." He proffered a metal bar from the stables. "Shall I open the box?"

Mira raised a halting hand as her gaze shifted inward. Her thoughts drifted to the Transylvanians who had seen fit to take her beloved from her. Perhaps some of these ignorant youths, or even Furlong, had participated in the desecration and inflammation. Other than Sterling, only one foreign face betrayed innocence. "No. Go and take your band of youths with you. Leave Igor. He is restored to my favored whim. Give him the box opener."

Igor accepted the tool along with a pitying look from his temporary master. As for his recent coworkers, they could not evacuate the room quickly enough.

Igor jabbed the thin wedge of the bar into a box seam and immediately paused at the Countess' outcry.

"Hold, you savage! First make note of the images on the exterior."

This required paper and ink, which took time to arrive. After establishing Igor's fat fingers could only copy the coffin at a limited speed, Mira drafted Sterling, whose representations proved nigh unintelligible. Finally, she took up pen and they completed their task two hours before sunrise.

"See the fancies curled around those images?" By this time, Mira had started sharing her third hand knowledge of hieroglyphics. "The encircling of the name means this is the sarcophagus of a pharaoh."

"The name appears to be two symbols," nodded Sterling, "the end of a pipe and a large woman next to a smaller one."

"It is a water dispenser, a spigot," said Igor.

Mira smiled benevolently at her students. "Exactly, and the second glyph denotes how special the enclosed mummy must have been. Vlad translated the name as Pharaoh Spigot Superior."

"They had a Ramses, didn't they?" commented Sterling. "A better faucet seems like a comedown."

Mira looked exhausted. "Have Furlong send one of his boys to my quarters," she ordered Igor. "I will rest. We shall finish this later." She departed.

"We won't see her before sunset," said Sterling.

"Do you believe the story of the Count's demise?" asked Igor with a shiver.

"She wears black or white," answered Sterling, "which is enough for me."

"Does her wardrobe contain any other colors?"

***

A stranger to Sterling and Igor waited in the sitting room when they reconvened at dusk.

"I am Dr. Lionel Lupo, and I have come to call on the Countess." The man bore himself with the dignity of an obligation. He managed to look graceful, stiff, and hungry.

"Please sit," insisted Sterling. "Our hostess will be down shortly, I expect."

"A strange mist hangs upon the castle grounds," said Lionel. "I almost turned back, but I have delayed too long in paying my respects."

The three of them contemplated the shambles of furniture and the large Egyptian coffin on one side of the room.

"We worked on the burial artifact last night," explained Igor.

The doctor disapproved though he said, "It appears to be an embarrassment of curiosity."

"Do you read hieroglyphics, Doctor?" inquired Sterling.

"I attended university in Germany, sir," replied Lupo. "No language is beyond the bounds of my training." He suddenly cocked an ear toward the door. "The Countess approaches."

"I would be interested to hear more of your personal history, Doctor," said Sterling.

"Like you, I am made up of moments encircled by a boundary," replied Lupo.

A minute passed before Mira entered in a long black gown, wound tight to her narrow figure. "Lionel."

The doctor paused, like a mouse awaiting a pouncing cat, but pulled himself together, "Mira." His face went placid from its momentary grimness. "I come bearing the condolences of our entire clan."

"Surely not the entire clan, Lionel?" She displayed her special smile, the one which exhibited her fangs.

"Claude is old, but the pack otherwise regrets Vlad's passing."

"Claude under a full moon must be a laughable sight." Mira sat. "I thought lycanthropes did not tolerate the aged."

Lionel leaned against the mantlepiece. "We are not barbarians, riding into these lands on Attila's coattails, bearing the rags on our backs and selling nightmares."

Mira leapt to her feet, "And Vlad could not be mistaken for a dog waking in a bed of offal and self-recrimination, unable to believe or accept his own mythology."

Sterling joined the others on their feet. "Friends! Can't we all get along?"

Unified for once, Mira and Lionel gave the Monster pitying looks, turned their backs on him, and flounced into the nearest chairs.

"It is good to see you are recovering from your tragic loss, dearest Mira," offered Lionel. "Have you identified the villain who admitted the people?"

Igor stepped forward, "I have made inquiries on the Lady's behalf. They have not borne fruit."

"I appreciate you tearing yourself away from your precious pups to call on me in my time of grief," accepted Mira. "Igor, have you freed the lid from the box yet?"

"Yes, Master," said the wayward assistant to mad scientists. He cringed, "Forgive me- force of habit. I am humbled by your notice, Mistress. Let me wield this bar of iron and free the contents of the sarcophagus."

"What a beautiful artifact," commented Lionel.

"I'm curious, Doctor," said Sterling, "Do you trace your line back as far as the Ancient Egyptians? I'm to understand Mira and Vlad do."

"You flatter me," said Mira. "Creating a vampire is a little different from human procreation. It is the second birth which draws a line into the past from time immemorial."

Sterling continued, "Even so, never having known sexual life-giving, I find the very idea of biological reproduction..."

"Or production," Lionel stomped his cane twice and laughed.

"Igor is little different," added Sterling. "He's had so many replacement parts I doubt he has had an original thought in decades."

Igor edged over by the fireplace. Holding the iron bar behind his back, he tilted the sharp end into the flames. "We both look good for our age," replied Igor to Sterling. "Lionel is the only one in this room who cannot lay claim to an unusually long lifespan."

"I would not trade one night running naked in the woods with all my senses fully trained," said Lionel. "Better than sitting in this room like a dilettante watching an endless life pass from a tower."

Igor crossed rapidly to Sterling and waved the red hot bar at the Monster's throat. "Go ahead and call me a fool again!"

Sterling struggled to clamp down his fear of burning, "Face it, we were both made for a purpose. It's not your fault you will always be drawn to the servant class."

Lionel pounded with his cane yet again. "Gentlemen! Life is too short!"

The other three looked at him. In unison, they burst into laughter.

Lionel left the protection of the edge of the room and ventured to one of the heavily padded chairs, French from the look of its legs. He took a moment to settle comfortably. Leaning forward, he rested his chin on the head of his cane,

"How old? A century?" he directed this at Igor. "The same?" he gave to Sterling.

Mira held up her hand, "A lady never tells."

"You don't look a day over thirty, my dear," said Lionel, "But we both comprehend how appearances can deceive." He sat back and gave them each a studied examination before continuing, "Do you recall what came before all of you? Wolves."

Mira looked bored. "Are you sure you can say the same for the contents of the box? The heart leaps with wonder at its age. Igor, if you wouldn't mind returning to your task."

"I live to assist." Wielding the iron bar, Igor attacked the coffin with renewed vigor.

The remaining trio watched, masking their interest with feigned indifference. Even Sterling had grown self-important in recent years.

The stone slid with a rough groan, signaling Igor's success. He waved them over, arranging each out of the way of the tipping lid.

"Stop!" rang a voice made of wind and anger.

"Beloved?" said Mira, searching the room, but finding nothing.

During the ensuing silence, Igor returned to the box.

The invisible voice announced, "You must not expose the mummy!"

"Do I hear Vlad's voice?" asked Sterling. "Where is he?"

Mira shushed the murmuring of the others. "He is disembodied. This is the only explanation."

"What sorcery is this?" asked Igor.

"We are capable of transubstantiation," explained Mira.

"Like a werewolf," grinned Lionel.

"No! ...yes," said Mira. "Vlad could have become mist in his dying moments. He has no way to feed or to gain the strength to return to his true form."

"Mumia can save me!" came the voice.

"That would be mummy dust," said Lionel.

"Do you require us to scoop a portion from the bottom of the coffin?" asked Igor.

"I'm afraid it is made by turning the mummy into powder," elaborated Lionel.

"But she was a gift for me!" declared Mira.

"She?" wondered Igor.

"A female pharaoh?" said Lionel. "How unusual."

Sterling raised a hand, "Even I am aware of Cleopatra."

"The Germans have a word for this level of discourse," said Mira, "kindergarten."

"I demand revival!" cried the voice. Wind rushed about the room, stirring papers and hairs, and raising a stench like mildewed paper.

"When Vlad had exhausted his harem of female vampires, he demanded sturdier playthings," explained Mira. "His seeking led him first to your late intended."

"My bride passed unexceptionally," commented Sterling.

"Vlad had hoped your creator could improve on his initial creations," said Mira. "He did not kill your would-be bride."

"I do not need improvement," responded the Monster before turning maudlin, "Frankenstein is long dead."

"Which is how this one," Mira gestured disdainfully at Igor, "arrived at our door. He is not the inheritor of his prior master's mantel."

"True," agreed the perennial assistant, "though call me neither slave nor servant."

"Nor savant," added Sterling. "What of those women who suffered at Vlad's hand?"

"I disapproved of his tormenting them into nonexistence so quickly," said Mira. "He turned on me then."

"Deconstruct the Egyptian!" yelled the air around them.

Frightened, Igor neared Mira. He held out the crowbar. "What would you have us do?"

Mira looked at the scared, self-perpetuating man who defied her terrifying, cruel, deceased husband. "Why petition me?"

"You are the mistress of the castle," answered Igor.

"The box and its contents belong to you," added Sterling.

"Actually," Lionel stepped between Mira and the sarcophagus, "another might have something to say." He nudged the lid with his hip.

Mira strode up to the werewolf, "You dare to claim a right of decision in my abode? Either you suffer from misapprehension bordering on madness or you are far more stupid than I previously imagined."

"I find your closeness enticing," retorted Lionel, "but I ought to clarify. I did not speak on my own behalf." He shifted slightly.

A hand clothed in linen wrap rose through a crack in the interior of the sarcophagus. Rotten fingernails poked through the cloth. Shifting and rocking emanated from within. Everyone in the room stepped back.

"Do not free the mummy!" cried the air. "I will not be doomed by such as yourselves!"

The coffin lid tumbled sideways to reveal a large corpse, in stained strips gone far to yellow and brown. As it bent at the waist, it groaned loudly enough to drown out the wind. It paused in a seated position while its spine released a horrific crack. A sigh like a broken bellows burst from within the wrappings and two strips drooped.

"It's alive," commented Igor.

Sterling went to the Mummy and helped it out of the coffin. A tinkle of glistening amulets fell from the bandages onto the floor. They resembled hieroglyphs, insects, and cats.

"Is she all right?" asked Mira.

"No! No! No!" echoed within the walls.

"What do you propose to do, Mira dear?" asked Lionel, simultaneously offering a hand to the ancient Egyptian.

The Mummy felt the doctor's touch and turned its head. The effort involved in the movement caused the wrappings to shift. Linen threads sprang up around the neck. Like eyelids, the covering spread wide to reveal the eyes fully. They looked dry, grey in the cornea, and awake. They blinked furiously and then scanned Lionel. The Mummy spoke in an unknown tongue.

"Mira, I order you to send this thing to the kitchens to be ground to dust!" The room quaked with the pronouncement.

Drawn by the Mummy's gaze, Mira moved closer and they stared at one another. "My husband was always a pedant. You'll do for now."

"Mira!" screamed the wind.

"Desist, Vlad!" retorted the Countess. "I have no intention of reviving you!"

"You can't mean it! I will find a way and return! You will pay for this betrayal! All of you!"

The candles in the room went out in a rush of air.

The room hung empty with the sudden drop in air pressure. Those who breathed paused until Mira spoke, "Igor, would you be so kind as to locate the matches?"

Nervously, Igor proceeded around the room. Once finished, he collapsed on the nearest chair. "What are we going to do? He'll find us."

"I find it difficult to fear my old friend," said Sterling.

"You should," said Mira, rolling up her sleeve to reveal a savage burn along the forearm. "He held a heated iron against me after securing me in my resting place."

"Why?" asked Sterling.

"He needs to be cruel," said Mira. "I only understood when he turned on me. I opened the gates of the castle to the townspeople with their torches and pitchforks."

The gathering sat in silent contemplation, not looking at one another.

Lionel broke the quiet, "I come in contact with cruel wolves. Perhaps we should keep one another's safety in mind. I can watch the lupine clans. I suspect, Countess, you have a similar power of oversight of your kind. Perhaps those of us here could alert one another if the wind should speak again?"

Mira nodded, followed by Sterling and Igor.

"That leaves the Egyptian," said Lionel.

"I will see to her," said Mira. When she saw the raised eyebrows on the others, she added, "With the proper training, she may make a worthy addition to our conference . With a little cultivation, she should be able to surpass Sterling and Igor in grace and you, Doctor, in personal strength."

GIL RETURNS A FAVOR

Alejandro stood under his grandfather's sign, Vulcanizadora La Laguna. He looked at his knuckles, as stained as they had been before he finished washing. He watched the street for the guest he had been awaiting every night for the past three weeks. This his grandfather Rubén had asked of him.

The occasional passerby looked past Alejandro and saw a pile of tires, shelved tools, piled wheel rims arranged like chairs. On such a cool night, the blue flame in the work oven might look inviting. Still, nobody on foot needed an auto mechanic, especially one specializing in tire repair.

Rubén and Laura raised four children here. The youngest daughter had moved back with Alejandro after her husband died. It had been a fascinating place to play, particularly on slow days, which proved to be most of them.

Alejandro rubbed the burn scar on his left arm. If they found a way to smooth it pretty, he would turn them down. He no longer remembered when he looked symmetrical. Hearing his name, Alejandro turned toward the small building which had served as home and office for generations.

Rubén stood in the doorway, a flash of blue light illuminating his face. "Has he come?"

Alejandro wanted to walk to the corner for a taco and to flirt with the young woman who took the orders. "I don't know this Gilberto. How am I supposed to recognize him if you won't tell me anything other than he's really big?" Uncertain if the old man even heard him speak, Alejandro walked across the empty work yard. "I want to go for a walk."

Rubén's eyes glowed, with the whites tinted blue. "I want your mother back. Nothing else."

"How is a stranger supposed to help?" Alejandro shrugged. "It's been two months! The police are useless! The federals are no good!"

Rubén turned back inside. "You should take your walk."

Later, Alejandro wandered home and paused at the fence gate. It had been dry all day, but somebody had left a puddle on the sidewalk. Scanning up and down the street, Alejandro guessed the visitor had come from Laguna del Coapinole only a block away.

Two hours passed before Alejandro woke on the sofa to find the television showing a muted football match on time delay from Spain. Outside in the yard, the cans on the fence rattled like a strong wind had kicked up.

Darkness filled the night this far from the tourist hubs. Tugging the door open suddenly, Alejandro saw a rat peer from beside a tire. He convinced the rodent to amble out of sight. Waiting a moment, he confirmed someone stood at the gate, large like Rubén had predicted.

"What?" called Alejandro without moving.

The gate cans responded vigorously.

"Go to bed!" yelled Alejandro, expecting to hear a similar admonition from his neighbors.

"Don't make me break this gate." The voice carried through the air like a whale's song through water.

Thinking he maybe should have brought the bat or the shotgun, Alejandro crossed to the stranger.

"Is Rubén around?"

"It's late. He's asleep. Come back tomorrow," replied Alejandro.

"Let him in," came a voice. Rubén stepped into the yard.

Shrugging, the grandson unlocked the gate and revealed a hulking shadow in a raincoat turned inside out. Alejandro looked between the apparition and the old man. "Grandfather?" he finally asked since neither of the others seemed inclined to move or speak.

"Mr. Sardonic, this is Alejandro." Rubén sounded exasperated.

"Still a comedian." The voice matched the old man's attitude.

"Still don't have a last name?" asked Rubén.

"Last names are for friends," replied the stranger, stepping through the gate and showing his face.

"Lay off my grandfather," protested Alejandro. "He's an old man and doesn't deserve shit from you."

"I'm older than he is," said Mr. Sardonic.

Alejandro studied his weird face, "Yeah, that tracks."

"Gil is here to help find your mother," said Rubén as though surprising himself with the information. "He owes me a favor."

"How's an old, goggle-wearing, bald dude with a bad complexion supposed to help us?" complained Alejandro. A heavy hand landed on the young man's shoulder, dripping water. Alejandro watched the fingers flex claws, definitely something more than nails.

"Those are not spectacles. They are his eyes," corrected Rubén. "Don't upset the fish man." He motioned for the other two to follow him inside.

As they walked, Alejandro dodged out from under the green hand. "You didn't have to soak my shirt. Did you swim here?"

"No one answered earlier, so I took a dip in the lagoon."

Alejandro stopped short of the doorway and turned on the stranger. Deciding he did not care what kind of monster he faced, he stared into those jewel-shaped eyes, and stated, "I don't suppose you came upon my mother in there. Because I really don't want to hear it. We are not going inside, sitting at my grandfather's kitchen table, and telling him his favorite daughter is lying down there. Do I make myself clear?"

"You have courage," replied Gil. "I can see why your grandfather is proud of you." When Alejandro did not make way for him, Gil explained, "He writes me one letter each year to remind me how I still owe him a favor. Over time, he has become more expansive. I imagine he does not have many people to talk to."

"Apparently more than he mentions," Alejandro went inside. "I've never seen him buy a stamp in my life."

Rubén had put out jelly glasses and a bottle of raicilla. He poured once all three kitchen chairs had been occupied.

He studied their guest. "Once your debt is paid, will we be friends?"

Gil considered and finally nodded.

"To future friends," said Rubén and banged their glasses.

The glasses had only reached the table when Gil asked, "What do you expect me to do about the missing woman?"

Alejandro lost his breath then. If this creature had nothing to offer, then why had his grandfather bothered? Suddenly the world rushed in on him. The pattern on the tablecloth became too complicated. His head became too hot and his hands grew too cold.

Then it stopped.

Rubén and Gil had each taken one of Alejandro's hands in warming grips. The palms of Gil's frightening green hands felt soft like well-tanned leather.

"Let's start again," said Gil. "Tell me how I can help."

***

Inez had been playing in the yard when Gil rolled up with a flat tire. Beneath the sign for the auto repair shop, Inez had tacked a less formal cardboard announcement:

Toy cars and trucks repaired.

Hours: Monday to Friday after school unless a better offer comes along

Payment: Pesos or trade/pesos preferred

"Nothing better come along today?" inquired Gil from the locked gate.

Inez eyed Gil much like her future son would. After putting her tools precisely down and resting the wheel-less model car on a nearby table, Inez approached. "You don't look normal."

"It's because I have a flat tire and I've been rattling my teeth for a half hour," Gil opened his mouth so she could see the proof.

"What's wrong with you?" Inez had not moved to open the gate.

"Is your daddy home?" asked Gil.

"Yep," answered Inez. "Tell me what's wrong with you and I'll go get him."

"How about if I go to the phone booth down the street and call the number written on the sign over my head? Will your daddy be happy then?" Gil watched Inez shake her head, more than a little disappointed in a world in which a little girl could not receive an answer to a simple question.

Inez turned for the building at the back of the yard.

"Stop!" thundered Gil. "What's your name?" asked Gil, more quietly and slightly more tenderly.

Keeping her back to him, she turned her head, "Inez."

"My name is Gil. I am different. And I don't know why." He did not smile because he could not carry the expression well with his facial attributes. "Can I speak to your father now?"

Inez returned after a few minutes trailed by a man between early and late middle age. His arms were clean enough but his shirt betrayed his workday. Gil explained his situation and they negotiated a price before the gate opened.

Gil said he would be at the lagoon at the end of the road.

A half hour later, Gil broke the surface of the water and found Inez sitting on a bench at the edge of the water. With arms crossed, she announced, "My papa says you are probably not going to pay him. I said I wouldn't have let you in if I had known. My papa says I can have a taco al pastor from the gringo place if you pay him." She studied Gil closely.

"Why do you want a taco from there?" asked Gil.

"Because they use the sauce from the supermarket and the tourists don't even realize," answered Inez. "It's different from Mama's recipe."

"Is it better?" asked Gil.

Inez considered. "It's different." Feeling she could be losing her argument with her only ally, she added, "I thought you liked different."

"Your grandfather is right," stated Gil.

"Because I shouldn't eat overpriced tacos made without love?" said Inez.

"I'm probably not going to pay him," corrected Gil. He walked into the shallows, revealing a lack of clothes, though scales covered anything inappropriate.

"You have bullet wounds." Inez slid off the bench and looked away.

"Bring me my clothes and you won't have to see them," said Gil. "A little girl shouldn't be able to diagnose scars."

Inez handed the bundle over her shoulder. "My Papa has one. According to Mama, he tells a different story about it depending on who's listening."

Gil chuckled. "I angered men and they had guns. I didn't. They left me for dead. The story hasn't changed in over two decades."

Inez decided he must have dressed by now and spun around, "You're not going to hurt my Papa!"

Gil held up his hands, "I promise." He headed for the road back to the mechanic. "I mean physically. I still don't have any way to pay him however."

***

Gil dragged two plastic chairs under the overhang by the rubber oven. After taking off the raincoat, he adjusted the chairs to support his extended legs as he sat. Then he draped the coat carefully across his exposed body. He could hear the conversation in the doorway, but he would rather sleep.

"Where are his parts?" asked Alejandro. "Is he a man or a woman?"

Rubén rolled his eyes. "You worry about unimportant things. He is a creature from far south and he drove a truck a long time ago. He had a breakdown and he stopped here. I helped him. Your grandmother fed him. He had no money. I accepted his IOU. He's no more special than you or me. Does any more than that matter?"

"I'm a grown man," protested Alejandro. "I could go after my own mother."

"Yes, but I don't have any more goodbyes left," answered Rubén.

"Why do you say such things? It's not what I mean." Alejandro studied the stranger dozing on their cheap furniture. "I wasn't alive when you last saw this man. My mother was little. That's a very long time to keep this kind of promise. Why didn't he send you pesos?"

Rubén placed a hand on his grandson's shoulder. "I don't believe a long time to you and me is the same as a long time to him. He never sent money because I never asked."

"Also, where did he come from? And where did he park? You don't suppose he left another broken truck out in the city?"

"He collects his mail in Baja. Otherwise, I cannot say," said Rubén. "Except for good night." He called across the yard, "To you, too, Gil!"

Gil waved to their backs.

"You don't suppose he swam here?" concluded Alejandro for the night.

***

Alejandro drove Gil to the last place Inez had been seen. They sat in silence until they hit the traffic congestion in Nuevo Nayarit. Their slow progression spurred Gil to speak, hoping to keep Alejandro awake. "It's been two months."

"Grandfather hoped the police could do something."

"What about you?" asked Gil. He pulled out his shirt and poured water down his chest. "It's too damn hot to be in a truck."

"I thought she'd call and say she had gone somewhere out of service. She made friends on the job. They traveled. I went to school up by grandpa so I saw her only on her days off. The resort let staff families use the pool, on special days. Of course, the city was different before Nayarit built their resorts. When I was little,..."

Gil held up his hand, "I don't want to hear about when you were little. Tell me about Inez's disappearance."

"She lives in the worker's compound, shares a place with two other women. Mama works in the kitchen. They make the food for all the restaurants, so she can be stuck late. She left after her shift, which her boss confirmed. The roommates say she never made it home."

"No other friends?" asked Gil. "Maybe she took off with a boyfriend?"

Alejandro looked nonplussed. "She's fifty four years old. And she's my mother."

"Are you saying her parts had stopped working?" asked Gil.

"Your fucking face makes it hard to tell when you're joking," said Alejandro.

"I'm never joking," explained Gil. "What's her boss's name?"

***

The tall stranger sat down on the smoking bench. "Are you Carmen Ortega?" The Espectácular Azteca Hotel, Spa, and Resort had niches like this hidden all over the grounds, the only places staff and guests met on equal addicted footing.

Relieved the guy did not try to bum a cigarette, Carmen nodded. The stranger looked like he could be from corporate.

"You manage Inez Macedo?" asked Gil.

"I did," answered Carmen.

Gil longed to be back on his boat, reading a book or fishing. He bought a television in the 1980's but stopped replacing it after they canceled *Murder, She Wrote*. He tried to channel his inner Jessica Fletcher. "Did you kill her?"

Carmen slid his cigarette into the stone repository and rose to his feet. "You are neither a guest nor an employee, sir, and I would ask you to leave before I contact the actual police."

Gil stood and loomed over Carmen. "Tell me what happened to Inez."

This creature no longer looked human. His expressionless face looked capable of anything. The raincoat rippled with muscle. A disturbance clicked in the stranger's hands- perhaps an array of knives. "I don't know anything."

"I however want to know everything," encouraged Gil.

***

Gil had the driver drop him at Piedras Negras International Airport, though the Creature did not bother to go inside the terminal. He found a bench by the door and waited.

According to Alejandro, his mother had recently started at a brand new resort. He and Rubén had only seen Inez twice in the three months since. The last time, she had complained about poor security at the workers' compound. She counted almost two dozen employees who had disappeared. No explanations circulated about firings or resignations.

Carmen admitted the HR department at the Espectáculo Azteca Hotel, Spa, and Resort had been lax at recording the massive influx of new hires. Officially, it looked like two people in hospitality had disappeared. This could be explained by desertion, which Carmen swore happened more than Gil would believe.

Carmen's break ended, but Gil persuaded him to tarry. Carmen sat with a long, shimmery arm across his shoulders. In fear for his life and his job, Carmen admitted the local payroll coordinator had an arrangement with a human trafficking cartel. The coordinator, Heberto, paid three thousand pesos for likely names for his operation.

The third time Inez asked about a missing girl from her building, Carmen offered her up to Heberto.

Gil thanked Carmen for being so helpful and held out his green hand.

Carmen thought the quickest path to freedom went through this handshake.

Gil crushed Carmen's hand and then placed a comforting palm over Carmen's face until the manager increased his break time with a nap. Gil let Carmen drop where he stood, which may have added a concussion.

Outside the airport, Gil suspected an approaching orange van aimed for him when he saw the Tennessee license plate. It did not screech to a halt, but it rattled disconcertingly. The passenger window rolled down and Gil leaned in. "How are you, Farrah?"

"You need more friends," answered the Mummy. "Climb in before all the AC leaks away! You don't want to see what sweat does to my wrappings."

As they pulled away from the curb, Gil commented, "You didn't drive an old rust bucket the last time I saw you."

"This one is borrowed," said Farrah, testing the shocks at the airport exit. "I would not bring my beautiful RV on this outing of yours. It's for road trips, not shenanigans. What happened to your truck?"

"Left it with a guy for a tune-up." A half hour passed. While waiting in line at the U.S. border, Gil offered, "I appreciate you doing this."

"Can you believe they call this the Camino Real International Bridge?" said Farrah. "Tennessee Williams would love to be here right now." She pulled a straw hat out from under her seat and made herself as presentable as her bandages allowed.

Even so, the first words from the border patrol officer had to be, "Are you all right to be driving, sir? Ma'am?"

Farrah lowered her sunglasses and batted her fake eyelashes at the young man. "It's a skin treatment. They only offer it south of the border. Can you believe I can't take these off until we reach Oklahoma?"

"Can't your husband drive?" asked the officer, looking across the front seat.

"George lost his license for driving while stupid," Farrah giggled, which sounded like plywood cracking.

The officer waved them through and wished them well with a courteous "Fuck me."

"You are a marvel, Farrah," complimented Gil.

***

The dirty white van drove through the mobile home park until it reached the back road. In the western corner, it veered off the pavement and off across the dirt. Weaving hard, it navigated through a dip and across to a dilapidated circle of motor homes. They looked like a historical display of the progress in mobile housing over the last thirty years.

The van stopped. A man came out of the up-to-date RV and met the van driver. They both carried guns on their hips and an attitude on their shoulders. They opened the back of the van and directed the occupants out and into the less sturdy structures.

Eight women, hunched and tired, did as dictated.

Back on the paved road, Farrah asked Gil to hand her back the binoculars. He shook her off and continued watching through the windshield. The van from the meat packing plant had passed right by Farrah's vehicle without a pause.

They had been in Texas for two days, tracing the smuggler's trail first to the receiver on the American side, the one who sent the trafficked humans on to their final destination. He had unwillingly explained his record-keeping system. Farrah spent two hours typing up his methodology so the police would be able to track down his victims once his body had been found in his truck depot office.

Gil and Farrah tracked Inez's path between the border and San Antonio, two hours by car. The meat packing plant sat on the big city's outskirts. Inez and the other members of the captive workforce had landed at this shithole RV circle under the oversight of one Randall Morris Heenis.

"Perhaps he was the driver?" asked Farrah.

"Probably," said Gil. His neck gills glowed red with anger, a sight the creature preferred to hide. "He'd want to be close on paydays, but he might prefer the job of sitting on his ass all day."

"He punched one of them," said Farrah.

"It's Inez," shouted Gil, already opening his door, which he immediately pulled shut as Farrah started the engine.

Their van lurched forward. They leaned hard into the turn onto dirt. Farrah barely navigated the shallow arroyo. The man abusing the women watched them approach. The other one ran out to stop them. He raised his gun too late to accomplish anything more than have his arm shatter before the rest of his bones as Farrah plowed through him.

Gil leapt out before Farrah forced them to a stop. Through the windshield, the mummy watched the drama play out. They had not stopped to weapon up, so Gil had no option but to close the distance with the remaining villain.

Heenis had the gun out as the intruders neared. His hand held steady. The gun flashed in the twilight. Heenis fired until he had exhausted his ammunition.

Gil lay on the ground, blood seeping from multiple holes.

Heenis took a menacing step back toward his captives, forcing them to cower. Then he stepped pompously over to Farrah's van. He sought the driver, but the front seats looked empty. Heenis walked around to the door and markedly pulled it open. He pulled a flashlight out and scanned the interior.

A finger poked Heenis in the side. "Looking for me?" asked Farrah. As Heenis backed out of the van, Farrah grabbed his gun hand and broke the wrist.

Heenis swung with the flashlight and grazed Farrah's head. She caught his arm on the follow through and wiggled until the forearm spun on the elbow joint.

Farrah let Heenis topple into her arms. Holding him on his feet, she slapped his face, "Don't go away now," she said. "The fun is only beginning."

Dragging the barely conscious Heenis by his ankle, Farrah checked on Gil. "The fish man needs water," she announced to the survivors.

Inez came and studied the creature. She crossed her arms and breathed a little heavy as recognition grew inside her. Inez shook her head hard to stop the emotion from bursting out of her. "Is that Gilberto?"

"Do you have any water?" demanded Farrah.

Inez drew the other captives from their shambles. A moment's direction and they brought out bottles and jugs, all near empty.

Inez crouched and poured the water into Gil.

"It's not enough," said Farrah.

A young woman ran out carrying a plastic bottle, "This is all there is."

Inez explained, "The Heenis makes a run every evening for supplies. He picks the girls he considers the best behaved to accompany him. They also get to eat and drink what they can on the return trip."

Gil opened one eye and whispered, "He's done a hell of a job making sure you're too occupied to save yourselves."

"I have been here only a short time," said Inez, "but already I've lost count of the days. Tell me Alejandro and Papa are all right?"

Gil nodded before passing out.

Farrah stood over the writhing Heenis. "Does he carry the keys to his van?" She patted his pocket until she located them.

The young woman with the water bottle took the keys from Farrah. "I'm the best driver."

When she heard, Inez's head snapped to attention. "Gilberto needs water. I don't know this one," Inez pointed at Farrah. "If these creatures could find us here, then they will find you if you don't come back."

Farrah and Inez watched the truck drive away. "Do you trust they'll come back?" asked Farrah.

Inez shrugged. "One of these other ladies can go knock on doors. Those idiots in the trailer park ignored this shit over here all this time. They can get out of bed now and do something." She studied the mummy. "You're not like Gilberto."

"No, I'm not."

"Are you his girlfriend?" asked Inez.

Farrah laughed. Standing over Heenis, she asked, "What should we do with him?"

"He liked his barbecue," answered Inez. "You should see the size of the smoker behind his RV."

***

They spent another week in Texas. ferrying the women to rides home. The young woman with the water bottle never surrendered the keys to Heenis' van, though she stayed until Farrah's van had been prepared for another border crossing.

Farrah drove Inez and Gil to Vulcanizadora La Laguna. They celebrated all night with Rubén and Alejandro. Gil and Rubén watched the sun rise after everyone else had fallen asleep.

"We tuned up your truck," said Rubén, leaning back on his chair and lighting his cigar.

"I'm not owing you another favor," said Gil, stretching his legs out on a hubcap ottoman.

"I only take cash," said Rubén.

"I have cash these days." Gil noticed how Rubén's cigar sagged a little. "Nobody writes me letters. No one ever did. You should keep sending them."

"You could write back occasionally," responded Rubén.

"Maybe I will."

"Maybe I'll have Alejandro drop you a line," added Rubén.

***

Inez did not return to the Espectácular Azteca Hotel, Spa, and Resort except to collect her back pay and give her notice. Conveniently, she found Carmen and Heberto together smoking in the cigarette grotto.

Carmen wore a sling and a heavy cast. Heberto stood when she approached. Neither looked pleased to see her.

"Don't go," said Inez. "I'm here to quit and collect my pay."

Heberto sighed with relief while Carmen kept looking around for Gil.

"Also, I'm going to need a list of all the people you sold," Inez stared at Heberto.

"There is no...," he protested.

Gil walked out of the nearby restroom and coughed.

Heberto and Carmen turned to go the other way but found Farrah on the path.

Carmen settled matters by saying to the payroll coordinator, "I don't want another broken arm. Can you even do your job without typing?"

Heberto slumped. "Anything else?" he asked Inez.

"I am not without a heart. I brought you each a gift." Inez held out two deli bags. "It's homemade jerky."

"Tell me, Heberto, how might we confirm you have a heart?" asked Gil and laid three sharp claws on Heberto's shoulder.

WE DID LITTLE GOOD TO EACH OTHER

The dog shifted vigorously in Igor's arms as he ran through the doors of No.3 Pembroke Studios in Kensington. He appeared more unkempt than usual because the renowned artist refused to meet Igor or his friends at his primary studio on the grounds of his Chelsea estate.

Hogarth Putterdam had risen far above his humble roots painting for pence in taverns. He had even graduated out of this humble studio through tenacity, personality, immense artistic talent, and even more aptitude for deal brokering. Still, he hung onto his friends from his pub days and every step along the way to the royal portraits which subsidized his much enhanced lifestyle.

Igor paused inside the studio entrance. Beside him on an easel, three miniatures dried. Each reproduced Putterdam's esteemed portrait of Queen Victoria's beloved spaniel, Dash.

The expert painter appeared beside Igor and inquired, "What have we here?" Before an answer came, Putterdam changed the subject, "I can't help satisfying my public. I have a man in the market who sells out of these little pictures as fast as I can paint them. I should have made my reputation as a printmaker, but we all don't want to be poor and filthy Blake mucking about with ink and type."

"They're like icons," said Igor.

"Clever lad," praised Putterdam. "You're always coming out with ideas, aren't you? Someone ought to put you to work bringing your thoughts to life." He lowered his gaze to the animal in Igor's arms and blanched. "Excuse me. We don't want the Countess to grow irritable. Perhaps you would prefer to wait outside with your, umm, pet."

"This is something I threw together once I heard you'd agreed to paint us into a group portrait," Igor grinned, showing a collection of fine teeth harvested from handsome mouths.

Back at his canvas, Putterdam smiled at his subject. Mira mesmerized him. "Please look this way, but perhaps not so intensely. I am attempting to capture your soul, milady."

Mira almost imperceptibly slouched. "If you do, then keep it. I have done without for a very long time."

"You do yourself a disservice, Countess," retorted the artist.

"Did I see Igor by the door?" Mira knew the answer. "He is an early riser."

"I must find the way to tell him to leave me for a few hours. I need to rest," complained Putterdam. "When I accepted this commission, I never expected such as yourselves to keep the hours of tavern keepers, bakers, and dockworkers."

"I never expected an artist to complain about late hours," retorted Mira.

"Darkness may work for the stage or the song," explained Hogarth, "but it is no friend to the visual artist."

"I would advise you to demand better pay if I did not fill the role of your patron," said Mira, resisting a smile. "How much you overcharged us. Imagine me encouraging malfeasance."

"Please adjust the Cane Corso, Countess. Her majesty lies in her profile."

Mira whispered into the dog's ear and it immediately moved as directed. "To say nothing of the profit you have made acquiring dogs for each of us."

"No one comes to Putterdam without a canine."

"If I'm not mistaken, they may leave you without one, however," noted Mira. "Berthe here looks awfully like the champion you painted last summer."

"An exchange of one dog for another," said Putterdam. "I did a service for Lord Asquith and he showed his gratitude by gifting me the bitch at your feet. She had outgrown her pup-bearing."

"Haven't we all?" Mira did not make it sound like a joke.

Putterdam applied himself to the work for a few minutes before pausing to mix a new tone. "It's a pity you don't own a dog yourself."

Mira looked past the easel. "A long time ago, I learned never to trust any member of the wolf family."

"Did you perhaps have a bad accident as a child?" Hogarth fixed a line on the canvas.

"Dr. Lupo is familiar with the tale. Perhaps you should ask him."

"Yes, he brought your commission to me for this painting, which incidentally I must compliment myself on." Hogarth placed his hands on his hips and marveled at his own talent. "The doctor is an interesting man in his own right."

"You should have met his grandfather." Mira studied the ears of the dog at her feet. "He taught me the danger of allowing a dog into one's home. They are an animal who often overreaches."

"Don't tell me you suspect our dogs of spying upon us," protested Putterdam. "I have spent my entire life around every imaginable breed and cross. They fight as readily as they preen, but never have I suspected them of the intelligence or of the inclination for espionage."

"I'm not saying it's all bad," said Mira. "More than once, Lionel Lupo has passed along a helpful word."

"You baffle me, Countess. Even so, my artistry will capture your intriguing mix of wisdom, ferocity, and naiveté."

"To say nothing of my beauty," to this Mira added a curtsy over barely disguised annoyance.

"My ears are afire!" cried Lionel Lupo, walking into the studio. "I must be the subject under discussion." He walked up behind Putterdam and examined the artist's progress. "You've captured her magnificently, Hogarth." The doctor looked across the room. "Don't take it as a compliment, dear. I meant the gorgeous friend to man at your feet."

"No accounting for taste, rogue," responded Mira. "What are you carrying? It looks like what a groomer uses to sweep off the floor."

Putterdam preferred to deal with either the Countess or the doctor but not both together. He took Lionel by the arm and steered him toward the door, while he spoke over his shoulder at Mira, "It's the latest rage. The breeders are going small. Besides, it is Her Majesty's favorite breed."

"In fact," Lionel swerved away from the painter and headed straight for the vampire. "I brought this little darling as a peace offering." He proffered a King Charles Spaniel, which took one look at his potential mistress and yipped for his freedom.

Stepping back, Mira released the Cane Corso at her feet. Then, she recovered and stood her ground. "Does the terrible thing have a name? I may want to call it when I'm next feeling peckish."

"I call it Ruthven," Lionel smiled, "like…"

Suddenly, Mira leapt upon the doctor. The pair tumbled across the floor in a flurry of snapping, scratching, biting, growling, and screaming.

Putterdam cried at them to stop. Igor burst into the room. His strange pet jumped out of his grip even as Igor charged into the fray. Within moments the Werewolf, the Vampire, and the Brute fell apart like a porcelain vase dropped on a hard floor and miraculously shattering into three uneven pieces, all akimbo and more dangerous in their simplification.

Each combatant showed their true nature: Mira frowned like an angry agent of Hell, Lionel sat on his haunches with an outstretched tongue, and Igor held halting hands up at the other two, still gripping one another for a second round. Igor wrenched the pair apart before tumbling to the ground again. The combatants sat on their rumps, angry, embarrassed, and disheveled. The power dynamic had shifted on the floor.

"I cannot have this behavior in my studio," hissed Putter-dam.

Igor rose first and dusted himself off. He neared the artist so Putterdam had to study his mouth as he spoke. The breath of the self-sustained man caused Putterdam's sense of smell to shrivel. "Kindly send the bill for any inconvenience to the Queen's personal physician. He sits over there."

"I very well know who Lionel is," declared the artist. "He served as one of my first patrons."

"You chose to execute this commission at your back road studio rather than in the comfort of your estate, sir," continued Igor. "Do not expect well placed but absent friends to assist you here."

Mira and Lionel had straightened out and stood at the opposite shoulders of their oddly misshapen companion.

"Could anyone explain the nature of the dispute so we might avoid it in...?" inquired Putterdam.

Mira pointed a finger at the doctor, "He bore a gift dog with an abomination of a name."

"I only meant to honor the father of your dearly departed husband," countered Lionel.

"Ruthven behaved like a demon! He taught only cruelty. Vlad deserted him once he saw he could be a different type of vampire."

Putterdam covered his ears, "Milord, milady, and you, sir, respect how certain conversations are not for all ears!" He sang *God Save the Queen* quite loudly.

"You surprise me, Mira," declared Lionel, "because I have it on the best authority Vlad has been seen in his creator's company just this Saturday."

"You lie!" cried Mira.

"To what end?" asked Lionel.

"Why do your kind always lie? You seek to...," Mira sensed the danger of the hour.

Noting the rising sun, Igor raised his hands once again. "Are you certain, Lionel? Because this is very bad."

Lionel nodded sincerely.

Igor nodded in return.

Turning back to Putterdam, Igor pulled the hands from the artist's ears which also stopped his singing. "Who suspected such a song bore so many verses?"

"I first improvised on the tune during my school days," replied the artist. "I should probably apologize for rhyming Victoria with..."

"We heard it quite clearly the first time." Igor bent down to pick up his dog. "Time is pressing, Hogarth. You must immortalize Fifi and me immediately."

Hogarth turned pale, but then smiled madly under the trio's steady gazes.

***

"You could accidentally step on the little beast," Lionel placed the tankards down on the table. He knew his effort to loom over Farrah would fail, but he desired her to dispose of Igor's abomination before anyone from the pack saw them in the beast's company. "He would accept it because he would have to."

"Friends do not kill friend's pets willy nilly," said Farrah.

Forlorn, Lionel sat. "It sounds as if it's not completely out of the question, at least."

Farrah patted his hand with her heavy, bandaged fingers, "A lady must always be prepared for a little mayhem."

"Thackeray?" wondered Lionel.

"The Old Bailey," said the Mummy. "People accept me most easily in taverns and courts. I don't mind since they are both so much more entertaining than the stage."

"I had hoped to scare the Countess into leaving for the New World," said the Doctor.

"Poor little werewolf always wants to make a scene," said Farrah. "Nothing can be settled without a little display and soupçon of dominance. Too bad our scientifically inclined colleague came out on top."

"Can you believe Hogarth posed him front and center? I don't want to look at a monstrosity every time I see the painting. If anyone was born a background character, it's that negligible undereducated man-child."

Farrah drank deeply. "And yet, some days he is the best of us."

"You offend me, Madam." Lionel studied their tankards. "And you have a way with ale which confounds all experience of womankind."

"You should let Thomas Cook show you my homeland. This is table water compared to the best my people brewed."

"Sir?" A man of sycophantic disposition moused up to their table. "My name is Warmbath. I come from his Lordship." He gestured with precision though still defying interpretation.

Farrah beckoned the man forward, "Another of your followers, Doctor? I had heard every pack needs at least one to do the others' bidding."

"You jest in bad taste. My world is England writ small. Each creature fulfills its birthright with pride and honor. You see before you the pet of a different house."

Warmbath bowed uncertainly.

"He comes from Ruthven," clarified Dr. Lupo.

Warmbath shivered, "If you please, sir."

"You are among friends; sit and tell us your business."

"No, sir." Warmbath bowed again. "I am to tell you my master would have you bring all Hogarth's subjects to Cutwicke Manor for a late dinner the night after morrow." Warmbath bowed a third time and turned to leave.

"Ask him if he means tomorrow night or the next," said Farrah.

Lionel raised an eyebrow and received a shrug from Warmbath. "He means what he said."

After watching the servant depart, the Mummy commented, "Good lad."

"He'll be drained to the last drop within the week unless the old coot remains too busy creating an army of mindless drones."

"Like bees?" asked Farrah. "Don't look surprised- I counted apiculture among my passions in life."

"Exactly," agreed Lionel, "except he calls them zom-bees. I understand he picked them up in the Caribbean while running his sugar cane interests when it became too difficult to replenish his supply of slaves."

***

Mira hesitated when the carriage door opened. "Are you alone? I had arranged to travel with Farrah."

From inside, Lionel offered his hand to the Vampire. "She agreed to ride in a cart with Sterling and Igor. They're bringing the dogs."

"What above Hell for?" asked the Countess, accepting the hand and taking a seat within the carriage.

"While I find your ladyship companionable enough, I hesitate to enter the den of any vampire without additional affinity."

"You misjudge Ruthven," Mira spoke sternly before accentuating her point with a toothsome smile, "and probably me."

Lionel considered this and sat opposite Mira. They spent the next half hour watching the passing landscape while remaining vigilant in their guard against one another.

"Have you spoken to his Lordship since his return from the West Indies?" asked Lionel, grown bored.

"No, he blames me for Vlad's disincorporation," answered Mira.

Lionel did not pursue the subject. "He hosted a garden party on the solstice. Perhaps this is your opportunity to mend fences."

"He did not include me in the invitation because he has my future happiness in mind." Mira's expression exhibited a strong preference for a quiet ride.

"He has developed a fondness for fish," proposed Lionel as a change of subject. "You should see how he has stocked the lake and added additional ponds."

"Ruthven has always been an outlier in our community. We do not generally pursue hobbies."

"Apparently he encountered interesting creatures in the waters of central America while on an excursion from his estate. He frequently toured the other islands and the great isthmus between the continents." Once they left London, darkness enveloped the interior of the carriage. Dr. Lupo likely talked only for his own ears. "One intriguing beast grew to the size of a man."

"Too bad the old collector did not transport such a thing across the pond," commented Mira. "Kew Gardens would have paid handsomely for a mating pair."

"The locals lived in fear of the giant fish. Apparently, his Lordship proved more than willing to slaughter as many as pleased his hosts."

Mira feigned sleep until her eyes suddenly became visible. They glowed as the back of the eyeballs shimmered and the iris glittered with her natural purple.

Lionel had never seen anything more beautiful. He leaned forward, mesmerized by his desires. The carriage jounced. Steadying with an outreached arm, the Werewolf broke from the trance. "You attempt to seduce me, Madam."

"I have no need to try, Doctor, with a subject so susceptible to a mere glance." She allowed him to pout in the corner for a quarter hour before adding, "Come now, sir. Let us attempt tolerance. You have not found me desirable in the past. I blame the lateness of the hour and the tedium of the journey."

"No doubt," agreed Lionel, though his look suggested a continuing aversion to her. For her part, Mira accepted no blame for the discomfort within their cabin for the remainder of the ride.

***

Ruthven looked like Gainsborough's Blue Boy- flattened auburn hair over pearl skin with plump lips and an I'm-pretty-and-you're-not-worth-my-time attitude. He delayed his entrance until all his guests waited a half hour in the drawing room.

His upper-class accent inclined all present to engage in proper introductions before re-seating themselves while awaiting their drinks. Once the servants left the room, the Vampire Godfather returned to his feet. He studied each face before speaking. "I am pleased you could all be here for such an auspicious occasion. When weighing a long life, I assure you it offers few occasions which can be described as elevating, especially to such a degree as this one."

Lionel stood suddenly and raised his glass, spilling cognac on the carpet, "A toast, I say, to special occasions." His review of his companions revealed confusion and not a single raised arm in return.

"Sit, boy," commanded Ruthven. His age showed as his anger flared. Reinstated to his beauty, he waved a wrist bent in forgiveness to the doctor, "Very well, we toast the night. After all, who am I to disappoint my messenger? We would be nowhere without the good mendicant's arrangements for the main event." Ruthven turned to Mira. "A toast to the Countess."

The parties present raised their glasses though with many accompanying sidelong looks.

"Now, if I might introduce a dear friend who has been staying with me for a time," stated Ruthven.

Opening slightly, a door became visible in the wall beside the fireplace.

"I daresay a son of my own heart, the Count of Walachia," Ruthven flourished.

Vlad entered the room to absolute silence. He looked older than Ruthven, grayer in the skin and yellower in the eye, but he had regained corporeal form. In previous centuries, he had favored a cane for ceremonial purposes, though now he leaned on it as he stepped. He displayed no other infirmity, though he looked like a man giving his best performance of vitality.

Lionel moved first, going to Vlad, and leading him to the only available chair, "Old friend, you recover better than I imagined."

"Your advice to the lord of this house has been invaluable to this end, Lionel," Vlad's voice sounded much weaker than when he last yelled at the assembled monsters.

Ruthven gestured magnanimously, "And Vlad owes his continued recovery to you, Doctor, for it would not be worthwhile or possible without the sacrifices to come."

Finding himself in the closest proximity to Vlad, Sterling rose to his feet with a grunt. "What is the meaning of all this, Ruthven?"

The master of Cutwicke Manor stepped rapidly to Sterling, who initially towered over him. In a moment and with the lightest of levitations, they faced one another eye to eye. "Am

I mistaken or was not my honored guest kind to you in your distress? Did he not offer you shelter when you reached your wit's end?"

"He used me to his own ends, like so many before him." Sterling gritted his teeth. "I found myself at the head of an army charge against men for whom I bore no enmity and on behalf of men in the thrall of a madman who used war to distract his people from their misery."

Vlad pounded his cane on the floor but did not speak.

Ruthven took in the entire party. "I am faced with a preponderance of factotums, apparently." He moved behind Vlad. "When I first heard what had befallen my dearest creation, I wondered at my own decision making. I had chosen to spread my seed in distant places, leaving these familiar lands to Vlad and his progeny. How could I have chosen one who allowed himself to be deceived by rivals, acquaintances, friends, and lovers?"

The ancient deceiver went to a massive wooden globe in the corner and spun it slowly. "You have no idea the wonders waiting to be found, to be exploited. Allow me to share it with like-minded individuals.

"I do not doubt you have questioned what brought you to my doorstep this evening. 'His Lordship must plan a horrible evening.' 'Magnanimous Ruthven has finally seen the value in befriending others with experience of the peculiarity of long lives.' In truth, my potential surrogates, I have invited you here to see what manner of future fills your dreams."

The youth who hid his years so well bent to the suffering Vampire and offered a hand of support. Vlad brushed it away. The pair of them went for the hidden portal.

Before the barely visible door, Ruthven turned, "No doubt, you are tired after your journeys. Consider my people your own. I bid you goodnight."

***

"Absolutely not," insisted Ruthven's minion when he caught sight of Fifi. "The master would never allow it. The doctor willingly surrendered his disgusting companions to our kennel."

"I don't doubt your kennel is a well-oiled means to an end. Why don't you ask your maestro?" said Igor. "Either I am a guest or I am not."

A large shadow fell across the subordinate. He did not look at the source. "We have a doghouse for special pets overseen by very attentive boys," he begged.

"Perhaps another time, but my creation is in a very fragile state." Igor wiggled the dog's paw in all directions. "Will I need to tell your Lord how you caused the overnight death of my... familiar? From your perspective, it might have... consequences." Igor grinned.

Whether the encroaching shadow or the view of Igor's disheveled grin inspired him, the factotum scurried off.

Farrah stepped from the hallway umbra. "Your fiend is not well?"

"My dear dog is designed, much like the retinue of a local tavern breed their poodles and wolfhounds, except I could not bear to wait for generations to pass." Igor squeezed Fifi to his chest and her head flopped precariously before popping up and licking Igor on the nose. And flopping down again, though definitely breathing.

Farrah and the much shorter Igor headed to their rooms. "I am glad you persuaded the others to allow me to hold a feline in our group portrayal."

Igor stopped and held a hand to his ear, "Did you hear an outcry?"

***

Sterling, Igor, and Farrah pounded on Lionel's door before breaking it down. Farrah and Sterling carefully pushed the hinges free of the oaken door frame and set the hefty slab of wood on its end inside the room. Only then did the trio turn to find Lionel sitting at the dressing table smoking a pipe.

"Damn stupid idea," the Werewolf tapped out the tobacco into an ashtray. "I wanted to deaden my senses. It should work on smell and taste, but not hearing, but the tobacconist gave me his most nauseating brand. We agreed it might make me dizzy enough to drown out sounds." He pulled on his dinner jacket. "I suppose you'll want direction regarding Mira's scream. I'm afraid this is my fault."

"What have you been up to, you wretched creature?" demanded Sterling.

"Have you ever noticed how deferential everyone is to the Countess? It's not the same, but I demand a degree of respect, also." Lionel walked to Igor and grimaced. "We will never be like the three of you." He bent over so he could look in the Permanent Assistant's wandering eyes. "You are unique, my obsequious failure, but you will never command an army of Igors." Lionel turned on Farrah, "You will never run at the head of a pack. And you, an assemblage of discarded parts, will never comprehend the thrill of standing before a gathering of your own kind."

"What have you done?" insisted Farrah.

"I command packs," said Lionel.

"Mira is a Countess," conceded Igor.

"But Ruthven commands hordes of vampires. We could have had a glorious war, but instead, he only wanted the return of his bastard. He required the blood of a powerful vampire. Our interests aligned."

"Even your grandfather would not stoop to such a betrayal!" yelled Sterling.

"Pray tell," by now Lionel had doffed his smoking jacket and donned his full evening wear, "who am I betraying? Vampires or werewolves? What else is there?" He walked to the unblocked doorway. "One of the things I find endlessly fascinating about humanity is each one insists on their individuality even as they so forcefully place everyone else in easily identifiable groups. This is a danger none of you need ever fear.

"As for people," spat the Doctor, "not only the underclasses and the nobles, but all of them, will eventually acknowledge the monsters among them. Born a werewolf, I am special. As long as humanity fears me, then I have nothing to fear."

Farrah grabbed his arm, "What have they done with Mira?"

"I imagine they are preparing her for exsanguination," answered Lionel. "No one performs such a task quite as effectively as a vampire. Now let go of me."

Igor shook for a moment before filling Lionel's field of vision. "You'd be surprised at how adept an obsequious assistant could be at draining blood from the living. But I'm always happy to learn new techniques. How about you show us to the laboratory?"

***

The life histories of Sterling, the manufactured man, Farrah, the mummified pharaoh, and Igor, the student of scientific insanity, had inured them to the usual horrors and most of the unusual ones. All three shared experiences of dismemberment with intent to hurt, painful application of fire and electricity, and dread-filled, dark, solitary confinement. Nothing about what they came upon bothered them. But still, they shivered because the draining of hope from the basement of Cutwicke Manor hit like a wall of ice. Even Lionel felt the descent of futility.

Mira swayed on the wall, wooden stakes protruding from her forearms. Her head hung heavy with resignation.

The reason for her surrender had to be Vlad, who sat on a stool before her. His posture shaped an inquiry. He did not look at his former lady nor turn at the approach of the monstrous party.

The absence of their host filled the room.

Sterling left his comrades to speak with Vlad. He stepped between the Count and Countess. They exchanged soft words though the vampire barely moved. He looked up once right before Sterling retraced his heavy paces to his friends. When they saw him up close, he embodied the despair of the tableau behind him.

"I can no longer bear the presence of these beasts," said Sterling.

"What did the Transylvanian say?" asked Igor.

"The only thing holding back his complete resurrection is Mira's demonstration of how much she loves him. Ruthven has retired until sunset, exhausted from his efforts at persuading Mira to undo her heart, figuratively and literally."

Farrah studied the widowed couple. "I will end this."

Lionel moved as if waking from a bad dream. "Don't interfere. I have gone too far in my effort to broker a peace with the king of vampires."

"You couldn't broker a peace with a fox terrier," strained Farrah.

"Once Vlad is restored, then he will owe me a life debt," insisted Lionel. "He will return to his power base in Romania and continue his horrifying ways. He will eclipse Ruthven once again and then I can call in..."

Farrah's strong arm lashed out across the doctor's face, bending the man's neck sharply to the side as the body passed five feet into the stone wall. Crunch followed crack. Lionel lay against the wall like a butchered animal in a leather factory.

"What have you done?" yelled Igor.

No one stirred until Farrah moved to examine the dead Werewolf. "They do not change in death."

"Not in that direction. They are always buried human, which is for the best since wolves do not perform funerals," said Igor. He turned to his other companion, "Sterling, don't you...? Sterling?"

Thick footfalls echoed from the darkness of a long hallway.

Igor looked in Farrah's direction, wondering what to do, hoping she would tell him to put down Fifi and leave, perhaps never stop walking. Independent decision making did not always come naturally.

"Put down Fifi," said the Mummy.

Here it comes, hoped Igor.

"And go find Sterling. These are his friends." Farrah studied Igor's feet as if their movement might express his understanding. "If you go now, you might catch him before he reaches the coast."

Igor did not put down Fifi until he reached the edge of tunnel darkness. The dog did not follow its creator. Instead, it whined and settled onto its haunches to wait.

"Igor imbued you with greater wisdom than I speculated," said Farrah to Fifi, who expressed her agreement by licking her nether regions.

Farrah sighed, which erupted from various seams in her bandages and sounded like an asp moving across a marble floor. She dragged a stool beside Vlad and gingerly sat. She had learned not to trust furniture since her resurrection, but this wood held.

Deep wrinkles covered the skin of the old vampire, as if etched into wax. He betrayed a bare minimum of consciousness. He displayed no sign of respiration or cardiac activity.

"I don't suppose you've gone ahead and died," said Farrah. "Can vampires die? Or do you enter a stasis like frogs? Of all of us forsaken beings, your kind always struck me as the most amphibian, unless Ruthven's tales of fish men prove true."

"I cannot cease," exhaled Vlad, "nor can I continue." His words came at an irregular pace. "Ruthven held me in vapor form as a lure for whomever might fall into his manipulations. The stupid doctor fell first. A pox on him for being the biggest fool in his line for generations."

"Your Countess doubted both Lionel and the Lord, but she tired of running from the thought of you."

"For many a decade, I have not had the power to torment her," confessed the Count.

They sat in silence until Mira stirred with a guttural moan. She raised her head, examined the stakes which bound her, and drooped.

Her movement did not go unremarked by the other vampire, "We are a pitiful picture, my beloved betrayer."

"You have never known any true emotion," said Farrah.

"My kind were never made for love," responded Vlad. "I attempted tenderness at times, but I mostly failed. She was not better made."

"Then she has changed," said Farrah.

Mira tugged on her pinioned forearms and screeched, "I am right here!"

The Count tried to stand but stumbled back onto the chair. He undid his tunic. "Do not pity me for what I am about to show you. I am a proud villain who has met another villain on unequal terrain. Ruthven stood on solid ground when he found me in the ditch. He chose to keep me humbled rather than face me returned to strength."

His open shirt revealed mottled skin in a familiar pattern.

"Do I see a cross?" asked Farrah.

"When he returned me to corporeal form, the devil's devil placed an iron cross beneath my skin. I burn unendingly, but in my weakened state, I fear I would not survive its removal without the saving grace of she who hangs upon the wall."

Farrah did not hesitate, "As she hangs upon the wall, I imagine she did not agree to your proposition."

"I require her demise," admitted Vlad. "I hesitated and Ruthven demonstrated his impatience."

"I will ask this only once," said Farrah, "would you have her set free?" She leaned forward when she could not hear his answer.

"No!" Vlad's voice came like a dying storm, with spray and the smell of bile and the promise of an everlasting life in the shell of eternal death. He staggered to his feet and trudged to his Countess, stopping with her subtly out of reach. He had been impeded. "You dare touch me?"

"I dare more," said Farrah.

***

Igor did not have the night vision of Ruthven or the other vampires. Moving slowly, he came upon the outline of a closed door behind which lay a lit room. If nothing else, he might find a portable light, so Igor happily discovered no lock barred his entry.

A storm lamp sat on a nearby table. Igor tested the heat of the handle and scanned the room for a potholder or glove. The walls loomed more distant than expected. Even stranger,

Igor smelled and heard a pool, such as about a fountain in a garden.

Turning up the flame within the lamp, a large steel tank became visible. Glass windows periodically granted views inside the water-filled container. A most unusual man swam within.

"What are you?" wondered Igor for this did not look like any other human.

The creature had the usual four limbs, but large opalescent scales covered the skin. The ends of the appendages might be feet and hands, but they served well as paddles also. Coming up to the window and looking through the glass, large eyes studied Igor. Its mouth moved as if forming words, but the steel and thick glass made it impossible to discern.

A hatch surmounted the tank and a simple bar secured it shut. Proceeding on the social calculus that the enemy of his enemy could well be a friend, Igor moved a chair from the table into position. He paused before removing the bar. He could return to Fifi, leave the manor, and forget all of these people.

Igor almost stepped down.

When he did wrench the bar from the hatch, he expected it to burst open with its angry occupant leaping forth. Instead, he heard swimming. Igor precariously climbed higher. Peering down the access, he saw the humanoid fish head emerge from the water,

Studying the creature above him, the swimmer spoke.

"I do not speak any of the Iberian tongues," responded Igor, "but if you want out, here is my hand."

The creature from the dark tank weighed more than Igor expected, but together they managed to extract him from his prison. They balanced atop the tank and rested before dropping to the floor with a squelch.

An obligation to explain teased Igor, "I came in here looking for my friend, a tall man with heavy feet and a stern expression. Did you see him?" They stared at one another. "I suppose he'll find his own way."

***

Sterling emerged into the library of Cutwicke Manor. He walked with a quiet step, but he found no one among the books until he saw the balcony. He recognized the shape of Ruthven. It proved easy to approach the glass doors and block any escape for the vampire.

"The sun will rise soon. Is Vladimir restored already?" the Lord of the Manor turned. "He hesitated so greatly I doubted he would ever do the necessary."

"When I last saw him, he remained bedraggled," said Sterling.

"I wish we had met sooner and under different circumstances," Ruthven stepped toward the monster, forcing Sterling to retreat further indoors. "I could have made so much more of you."

"I am sufficient," said Sterling after a pause for thought.

"One of the many interesting things about being a vampire is our complete lack of doubt. We never require a brief interlude before declaring our worth, our intentions, or our feelings. We are never wrong."

"Vlad and Mira might disagree," said Sterling, now backed to the center of the library.

"Call me faithful to my kind, but I believe one of them will come out of this restored to their true strength." Ruthven lowered his gaze from Sterling's eyes.

The Monster sagged but the vampire's eyes drew him back as soon as Ruthven returned his focus to Sterling.

"Like you, so well-rigged and sturdy, you could amount to something if you surrendered your will to me," Ruthven smiled wanly. "It's not all about blood with us. I've collaborated with so many willing mortals over the centuries. I don't make demands or promises. Truly, it is all about a meeting of the minds. Was it Goethe or Spinoza who elevated such a connection to true love? Don't you agree, my poor, lonely man?"

Sterling screamed when the vampire extended a hand for the fingers suddenly appeared so long and sharp. The noise in the library quavered like a moan of terror.

A new sound broke through the concentrated evil in the room- a dog's bark.

Ruthven turned away from Sterling to face the confabulation of Fifi. The dog charged and bit the shin of the vampire before dashing through the French doors onto the balcony. Ruthven forgot Sterling and pursued the pooch, which he easily cornered by the stone railing of the porch.

Sterling slammed back to reason. He followed the two combatants but stopped before stepping outside. The arc of the sun appeared on the horizon. Sterling flung shut the doors and threw the lock.

Ruthven had grabbed Fifi, but when he looked out on the world, he saw the expanding golden arc. In the time it took him to raise a fist to shatter the glass of the doors, rays of light reached his midriff. His skin bubbled and blackened. The great villain's strength evaporated even as he clutched Fifi.

Sterling waited as Ruthven burned away to ashes floating on the wind before unlocking the doors. He stepped to the fallen dog, burned wherever she had contact with the fiery flesh of Ruthven. He petted the dying combatant.

***

In the basement, Igor turned the corner to find Farrah and Vlad in deep conference before the still trapped Mira. He scanned the corners of the room. "Where is Fifi?"

Before any response could come, Vlad arched his back and stood taller, looking strangely powerful. Farrah stumbled backwards as an aura briefly surrounded the restored vampire.

Vlad bared his teeth. "Who's not here?" He spun in a rapid roll call. "So, Sterling, my old friend, has eliminated the old devil who tormented me ever since blessing me with this cursed existence!

"Give me time to absorb Ruthven's demise and I will dispose of my pitiful Countess." The Count stepped toward Farrah. "You condescend to touch me? To patronize me? Do you treat me with pity as a serf fallen exhausted in the field? You, whom I once purchased from the Valley of the Kings. And what do they send me? A queen of unknown dynasty barely worth the effort of crushing into powder?"

Igor shuffled cautiously behind Vlad and tried to stir Mira. She raised eyes, grown milky as her effervescence drained away. Igor grasped one of the stakes and tugged until it came free. The Countess tumbled forward even as her eyes fluttered. She gave no recognition, though she did find her feet. She pawed at Igor and then her free hand sought out the stake still pinioning her to the wall.

Farrah raised her arms in anger over Vlad and rose to her full height. "How dare you lavish scorn on me!"

The Count grabbed her outstretched hands and spread them wide, raising terror from the mummy's desiccated heart. "You never imagined the power of a vampire lord."

A wooden stake erupted from the center of Vlad's chest. He had only a moment to complain, "Oh, consecrated crosses, garlic cloves, and parsnips..." The dread vampire burst into a flame which dissipated as quickly as it arrived leaving meandering strips of burnt flotsam sinking to the stone floor.

The stake dropped loudly to the ground.

Farrah looked at a relieved Igor who remained in his striking place.

"I... did," said Igor.

Farrah rushed to embrace him. "You are a wonderful, hideous whatever you are!"

Slowly they separated and looked at Mira, who considered them from her place at the wall.

"Am I next?" Mira heaved.

Farrah hurried to her, "No, no, no."

As the Mummy worked to free the Vampire, Mira pointed behind Farrah. Pausing at her labor, Farrah turned to see a strange Fish-like Man standing in the opposite corner of the room.

Gil mimicked the mummy's words until Igor went to him. Shushing, Igor explained, "I discovered him in a tank."

"Are you one of those creatures Ruthven found in the Americas?" asked Farrah.

"We need to return him to his home," said Igor, over the creature's insistent chant.

Mira ripped the remaining pinion out of her arm, staggered, and raged, "You killed my Count!"

Farrah tore her attention away from the creature and blocked Mira's unsteady progress.

Igor grabbed the creature by the scaly arm and escorted him to the secret passage which led above ground to the second floor. Hours must have passed since he had descended with the others to rescue Mira. Arriving upstairs, sparkling daylight surprised Igor.

Sterling perched on the bed, holding a soft bundle.

Sensing what his friend clutched, Igor moved at the pace of aching until he stood close enough to verify his fears. He extended his shaking hand to touch the furry head. After a tentative fingertip, Igor slowly moved his whole hand to caress gently what had once been his Fifi. A few moments later, he shifted the head back and forth, studying the joint. "We should find the kitchen and pack her in ice."

Sterling considered the moist eyes of the much smaller man. They shared a history in anatomical construction. "I cannot assist you further than carrying your creation down-stairs."

"You," Igor turned to the Fish Man and placed his dog's corpse into those sleek, glistening arms. Over his shoulder, he told Sterling, "I never let anything you cared about die." He turned and conducted dog body and creature from the room.

Sterling sat until he no longer heard footsteps from the hallway. He understood nothing of inheritance, but this bed felt softer than any he had slept in. The entire manor would benefit from redecoration. Perhaps he could stay and wait until an objection arose.

***

Down in the basement, Farrah mostly propped Mira up though she also kept a firm grip on the exhausted vampire.

"You're no less guilty in the demise of my love," spat Mira.

"Let them make for the coast. If they reach a ship, then you will never encounter Igor again," said Farrah.

Mira shrugged free of Farrah's grip. She stepped to the dead werewolf on the floor. "This pleases me. Your work?"

"Does it matter?" said the Mummy.

But the Vampire had already crouched to extract what she could from the Doctor's veins. Then she went for his marrow. By the time she finished, Lionel lay folded and piled amidst a scattering of rags. "I want to kill you. I want to start anew without any familiar faces. We have been only torment and oblivion to one another."

Farrah moved to embrace Mira, but in her hesitation, the Vampire moved to the secret passage entrance.

"Don't look for me," said Mira before vanishing.

This New Year's, Gil Will Entertain Alternative Opinions, Brian Will Wear A Suit, And Lionel Will Meet A Nice Girl

"I need water," Gil said to Farrah, since she was driving the mobile home. He didn't add that the thought of listening to the Progressive Radio Network for another minute had drained him of the will to live.

Farrah adjusted a few wraps with her free hand before turning off the radio. "Of course, you do. We're near Athens, a college town, and they have a river."

"And a bite to eat," added Gil. "I miss my lagoon." He undid his seat belt and headed for the lavatory, sidestepping the coffin in his path.

"I believe I strapped Mira down well enough but watch your step," Farrah heard a pained grunt behind her, "She can shift suddenly."

By the time Gil returned to his seat, they had pulled into a strip mall right off the highway exit. Farrah stood outside in the parking lot. A passing car slowed as Gil joined her after pulling on his new winter coat. "It's the latest in cold weather gear from fucking Patagonia," yelled Gil, prompting the car to accelerate away. "This is the price for traveling with a mummy. And leaving Baja."

"You're one to talk, tall, dark, and ornery," Farrah tweaked his scaly ear. She turned and headed for PetSmart. Gil shrugged and followed.

By the time they returned to their ride, Mira sat on her coffin picking at her teeth. "Buy anything worthwhile?" she commented.

Farrah held up crickets, "A queen has to eat."

Gil held his baggie overhead and poured three goldfish down his gullet. In a moment, he grinned and asked, "Did you eat?"

"A snack," said Mira. "Arteriosclerosis made it a little chunky. Did you hear? Lionel is bringing a date. Igor called to forewarn us."

"Futile and stupid," complained Gil.

"It's sweet," said Farrah. "He's the most likely of any of us to sustain a relationship. Besides, it's the time of year for making changes."

"Apparently they met in the woods one morning," said Mira. "She went out jogging or something equally ridiculous. He woke up beside this young man whose throat he had slashed. They bonded while hiding the body."

"Sturdy girl her," commented Gil.

***

"I suggest you leave the hooded sweatshirt on," said Igor.

Brian the Zombie held a bundle of clothes selected by his companions. "We promised to return the hoodie, but nothing is between me and it."

Sterling nodded, "Best to burn your previous garments, though preferably far from me."

Brian felt airy down below. He stumbled toward an unused shopping cart and used it to carry his bundle and hide his waist-down nudity. "I believe they have dressing rooms this way."

"I truly do not understand," said Sterling. "The old navy I knew never cared if you changed clothes midship. Privacy became a luxury on board." He gestured at a nearby employee and yelled, "How do any of these uniforms represent the navy? Is it a jest? I have traveled on great sailing ships." He moved toward the sales clerk, "Let me tell you about the time Captain Walton marooned me in the arctic..."

Igor followed the Zombie to the dressing rooms. "This is going to be so good for you, Brian. You can't go to a soirée and be all 'Blaha, undead walking here.' You need to dress to impress."

"But...," Brian shambled to a stop outside the dressing rooms before turning on Igor, "I'm not like you guys! I am aware what a department store is. I used to shop at Two Guys before all this happened to me. No one goes here to prepare for a fancy dinner at the Edison Hotel in Manhattan."

Igor scratched a mole off his cheek and then licked the blood from his finger. "Remind me to stop for a spool of thread at Joanne's later." He sighed, which started as a whistle deep inside. "The thing is, Brian, it is very difficult to acquire a nice suit in your size on short notice. Perhaps if you had taken better care of yourself..."

"It's called bloating!" responded Brian. "It happens after we die!"

Igor placed a contemplative finger under his chin and studied Brian. Then he wandered away.

Gathering up the clothes, Brian muttered, "'Let's prepare you for the big night, big guy.' 'We know what'll fix you right up.' 'Well, look who's all alone again.'" He chose the dressing room at the back where the lights flickered. After he had discarded half his choices, the electricity suddenly settled down.

"I'm just attaching something to the electric panel that will reduce you at least three sizes." Even through the door, Igor's voice slurped, "Honestly, I had a tougher time keeping one idiot scientist in AC/DC when he wanted to reanimate a cousin for Sterling. The mall electrician has a lot to answer for." He tapped the door. "I had a thought, Brian. Why don't you open the door and let me show you?"

The zombie mostly untangled from the shirt around his neck and popped the latch. He observed Igor holding an air pump with attached needle. Brian sighed, causing a boy to run out of the next dressing room and call for his mother as he scampered out of sight. "Will it make me more attractive?"

"Indubitably," reassured Igor. "Afterwards we can exit this purveyor of fool's wear and head for the Men's Wearhouse."

"I like the sound of that."

***

"You picked the place, Gil," said Mira.

"No, I said we should eat at a diner. I like local places. You meet real people." The creature encompassed the restaurant with a gesture, "But these are the same brainless youth we hear about all the time."

Mira held up thin fingers with long dark nails and counted, "No, you said we should stop at the first diner we saw. It's not our fault this is a Bob's Big Boy. Second, it is after midnight and these are the same drunken youth we hear about all the time, not necessarily their more thoughtful peers. They are stopping here after the bars in town have closed."

Farrah made the wrapping on her face wrinkle. Her voice audibly smiled, "Listen to the ideas of the future bubbling over all around us."

"Mostly I hear hangover cures being discussed. What sort of university do they have in the Appalachian Mountains anyway?" Gil stopped talking because their food order approached.

Once the waitress departed, Farrah dumped her bugs onto her pasta, using her fork to skewer any which escaped the plate. Mira stirred tomato juice, while squeezing a dark red liquid onto a celery stick and licking it off. Gil tossed the buns aside from his fried fish sandwich before scraping off the lettuce, tomato, and tartar sauce. Daintily, he nibbled on the slab held between two fingers.

They noticed the inevitable attention directed their way. The students at the surrounding tables had stopped eating.

Half the wait staff leaned against the counter and watched the trio of oddballs.

Gil gulped.

Farrah buried her bugs under the pasta.

Mira sat up straight and announced, "Have none of you ever seen a visiting professor eat before? Forgive us if our customs strike you as unusual."

Gil's eyes narrowed, "Mira, I feel judged for being different."

Many eyes dropped to their own meals. More circumspect, the wait staff returned to their tasks, but kept an eye on how much clean up might be required later.

Three students found their bravery and gathered tableside near Farrah. They asked what the trio of foreigners taught. Unsurprisingly, they replied Ancient Civilizations, European History, and Nautical Engineering. The latter amazed them due to their Midwestern location, though it did not hinder a lively political discussion once Farrah invited the youth back to the mobile home for beers. Her people had invented beer after all.

***

Igor steered the GMC Sierra erratically into the I80 rest area and parked sideways across three spots. The bed topper popped open, emitting Sterling and Brian. "Nice job covering all these lines on the pavement," commented Sterling. "From the looks of the other vehicles, you chose originality over blending."

"You're lucky I could keep us on the road," countered Igor. "I'm guiding this monster truck with a learner's permit." He caught a look in his companions' eyes and clarified, "I don't mean monster in any pejorative sense, of course- merely a positive description of its passengers, speaker included."

"I am not loud," Brian said to Sterling, "and I don't run over things."

"We would not be in such a hurry if we had not caused such a commotion at the mall," Sterling said.

"I apologized before we left Monroeville, but I had no idea I contained so much gas," explained Brian.

"I'm not blaming you," said Sterling. He looked at his huge shoes.

"How could I tell he contained a potpourri of pungent vapors?" asked Igor.

"I am decaying," clarified the Zombie.

"They had to evacuate the Old Navy," said Sterling.

They stood by the truck, refusing to look at one another.

Finally, Brian spoke, "At least we found the suit store empty. They even had my new size."

"You do look good in green silk," admitted Sterling.

"It offers camouflage for your pallor," added Igor. "Of course, we still would have been fine if Sterling had not lost his mind in the Men's Wearhouse. Do you always have to go for the shiniest thing in the room?"

"It's not my fault tie clips are so difficult to hold with these fingers," Sterling held up massive pro basketball hands. "The clerk had no right to clip them to my tender tips."

"He behaved extra mean," conceded Brian.

"He didn't need to have his arm torn off," said Igor, "publicly."

"Potato, tomato," sulked Sterling.

A child in the back of a Toyota Corolla waved vigorously as she passed. Only Brian noticed and he waved sweetly with his index finger, "I could eat you up," he said.

"And Doctor Pretorius wept!" exclaimed Igor. "The whole point of us making this unendurable road trip is so you can be presentable when we arrive at the Edison Hotel. What is it you kept saying all day on Christmas?"

The Zombie stared at the asphalt, "I want to be a real boy."

"To be fair," Sterling said, "he only started in with it after Mira put *Pinocchio* on the big screen to entertain the main course."

Igor punched Brian in the arm, "Who has your back? You want to look sharp for New Year's Eve. We want you to look sharp."

***

Gabe could not stop the shaking, not even after Mira drained him a little and tried hypnotherapy. "But capitalism disenfranchises the majority in favor of the minority..." He could drown in those huge dark eyes on the fish man.

Gil nodded, "Calm yourself, son. It's not your fault my friends want you to plant new ideas in my deep lagoon brain, thick from all the water pressure, as Farrah frequently reminds me. I'm sure you were the smartest boy in school back in... where did you come from?"

"Gates Mills," trembled out of Gabe's mouth.

"You're adorable," reassured Farrah. "Gabe, you should be very proud of yourself. You have outlasted your classmates by a solid forty minutes. Honestly, the first boy could barely put a sentence together."

Mira leaned in, "We had to demonstrate our seriousness about the eating of fingers."

Gabe managed to say, "Joey played the piano."

"Live and learn," admitted Mira. "We should have opened with the history major. Once she denied our existence, the conversation proceeded downhill."

"Good eyeballs on that one though," said Farrah, slurping up the remnants of an orb nog. "The viscosity really holds the vanilla."

"I told you," said Gil. "The orchid-ness really blooms." He turned to their surviving guest, "My friends have spent this endless highway trip attempting to convince me American college campuses are filled with young minds longing to de-bate serious issues. All I have done is insist the stakes be sufficiently inspirational."

"I'm not good under pressure," screamed Gabe. Suddenly fearful, he added, "I'm sorry. I didn't mean to yell. Or insult people who live deep in the ocean."

"It's a lagoon," said Gil, drily.

"I had higher hopes for the pair of professional debaters in Bloomington." Farrah fingered an iris out of her glass and nibbled at it. "You remember? They sat at a table with a sign: 'Communism is the answer. Convince me I'm wrong in ten minutes or less.'"

"They should have been better prepared for the history of the Soviet Union," Gil said. "Despite their failings, I'm glad we stopped draining a pint for every failure to remain on topic. It deteriorated the level of discourse too quickly."

"I experienced a good night," Mira smiled at the memory.

"Gabe, as the monster on the other side of the table," said Gil, "I am going to extend an olive branch. My experience is limited, but I have seen the benefits brought to my home by capitalism. I own a houseboat. Instead of spending my days seeking sustenance, I can trade my skills for food and have time left over for reading *El Financiero*."

Gabe hung his head and studied the bloody hand towel wrapped around his left hand. Maybe his fingers could be reattached? Then he remembered how his stomach would need to be pumped first. The nausea rose again. He pressed the towel against his mouth. It smelled like saltwater and solder. "Yes, capitalism has definite benefits," he removed the bulky hand from his mouth, "but it succeeds best when a level playing field exists. Democracy has proven to be the best counterweight to the deregulation preferred by business interests. When equal in power, democracy and capitalism both thrive, but the weakening of one leads to the ruin of both."

Gabe gagged for a moment, but suppressed whatever filled his mouth before continuing. "On the other hand, communism may present viable arguments, though its dialectic fails to account for individual autonomy in any useful fashion. Essentially, it ignores free will in favor of the inevitability of history." His brow wrinkled and his face flushed. "Maybe Sartre or Kant or..."

Farrah and Mira smiled at Gil, who had leaned back with a large exhalation. He looked past Farrah through the window at the sunrise. Only when Gabe vomited on the table did Gil return his attention to the present. "That looks like a knuckle right there." He studied Gabe approvingly with his big dark eyes. "Let's get you out of here."

Mira and Farrah cheered.

***

The Edison Ballroom is proud to announce we will once again host our annual New Year's Eve Gala! Michael Tesla and the Edison Big Band mark their 15th consecutive appearance at the gala. Michael has been entertaining audiences for many years with his special sound, traveling the world performing with the likes of Dean Martin and Mel Tormé. Michael's big band is composed of a 16- piece orchestra plus vocalists. Also featured at this event will be the romantic Latin sounds of the Increíble Baile Desatado.

***

Mira walked up beside Lionel, following his gaze to the dance band performing on the stage. "You wear a tuxedo well."

"Denise insisted. I thought she and I would be dancing with one another."

"Where is the lucky lady?" asked Mira.

Lionel pointed to the stage. "Backing singer in the middle."

"She is hot," said Gil, joining them.

"I practiced the samba and the merengue and the mambo all month," complained Lionel. "I've never had a girlfriend."

"Killer band," said Farrah dancing up beside them.

"How do you move so well?" asked Lionel.

"Where have you been keeping such a gorgeous dress?" demanded Mira.

Farrah took Lionel's hand, "Did I hear someone say mambo?"

Left alone, Mira looked at Gil. Gil looked at Mira.

"Nyah," they agreed.

"Would you like to talk about why the band's name does not match the initials on their instruments?" asked Mira.

"I would enjoy it very much," said Gil.

Soon enough, three large men stepped onto the dance floor. The band played a merengue. Mysteriously, these large bodies in faux silk suits moved in hip shifts and precision toe placement across the room and stopped before Mira and Gil.

Gil nodded, while Mira said, "Ziua de Anul Nou, Sterling, Igor, Brian. You found enough rayon to clothe you all."

"We look awesome," declared Brian.

"He stopped for a bite at the Salvation Army," explained Igor.

The music stumbled to a halt even as Sterling shook his hips in greeting Mira.

A man at the side of the stage yelled at the musicians, "Miguel is in the alley! Dead!"

All of the monsters hung their heads. Farrah and Lionel strolled back to their friends, frantically swinging their arms in a parody of innocence.

"Which one of you morons did this?" hissed Farrah, focused particularly on the new arrivals.

The silence lingered as they exchanged glances for quiet second after quiet second.

"It couldn't have been us," stated Igor. "We remained together the entire time."

"You said you left Brian alone for a snack," accused Gil.

"We made a pit stop at the Salvation Army in Weehawken across the river," responded Sterling.

"Honestly, it wasn't me," said Brian, "and I haven't seen these guys hurt anyone since Scranton."

Harrumphing, Gil said, "None of us either. I've been with Mira and Farrah for days, such long days."

"You truly expanded your horizons," said Mira.

Farrah turned on Lionel, "Well?"

"Well, what?" asked Lionel.

"When do we meet Denise?" demanded Farrah.

Lionel looked at the ceiling, maybe hid a tear, and then said, "The band's all cleared off. I suppose we can find her backstage."

As they filed toward the door, Igor hung back to walk beside Lionel, "Why so down in the mouth, Wolfman?"

Lionel shrugged, "For once I'd like to be considered like everybody else. I do my share of random killing, too. Werewolves are more notorious than any of you."

"I would not let Mira hear you posit such a thought," said Igor, causing Lionel to stop in his tracks and study the Vampire's back for a sign of any response.

"If I can't fit in with you guys," said Lionel, "then maybe I could be a normal man with a date. This is why I bought all our tickets."

Gil placed a hand on Lionel's shoulder, "You paid? I need to have a word with Farrah."

Igor frowned, "This is a benefit for The Actors Fund, I believe. It's good to give back. Who has benefited more than us from people walking home alone after a late night shift in a restaurant on Broadway?"

They found Denise alone in the Green Room assigned to IUD. She wore a tight dress over black leggings. Soon as Lionel appeared, they rubbed up against one another for reassurance.

Brian leaned toward Farrah, "How did they meet again?"

The bandages around her mouth made Farrah grin like a cold yeti. "He woke in the woods after the full moon and saw her, sitting on a nearby log, watching him sleep."

"Fully clothed?" asked Sterling.

Farrah nodded, "She even had a hunting knife to protect him while he recovered from his lunar romp."

Mira leaned into their klatch, "Good thing she happened to pass by because the state patrol had been searching for a missing local girl. Denise understood all about it and helped Lionel perfect his alibi before they headed home."

"As I heard it," said Gil, "they went back to his place." After seeing how Igor and Sterling looked at him, Gil added, "I like a good telenovela, especially a true life one."

Igor looked at Mira, "You did well getting him off his boat."

"We wanted to help him become less one-dimensional," nodded the Vampire.

Denise pulled away from Lionel and tugged the Werewolf over to his friends. "I've heard so much about all of you! I've known you my entire life!" She went down the line exchanging hugs and air kisses.

"I love a good buffet," said Igor, slipping to the side table.

Official-looking people dashed past in the hallway.

Sterling stepped out and stopped a passing stagehand, "Any word on the poor soul?"

"Now there's two!" announced the distraught youth before rushing off.

Denise placed her hand in Mira's, "I've always specially admired your work."

Mira raised their joined hands and sniffed, "You've been naughty recently."

Denise made an "Aw, shucks" smile, "I like to dabble."

Lionel walked up with a tiny plate of chicken wings. "Are you two making friends?"

"Lionel, your darling lady friend plans to boast to us about committing these backstage murders tonight," said Mira.

The three of them watched Lionel's wings tumble to the floor.

Brian approached, picked up the pieces, and ate them. The silent, concerned looks which greeted the action prompted the zombie to say, "Three second rule?"

"My girlfriend is a serial killer," said Lionel.

Farrah leaned in, "Pardon my eavesdropping, but is she really?"

Denise backed toward the mirrors, "I always wanted to join your ranks, but what's a poor girl from Racine supposed to do? I wasn't gifted with an epic back story! My parents worked for the city! But I loved you! All of you! I took weekend trips to Chicago while in high school. I practiced where I could. I have killed so many people! But no! None of you ever noticed! I had to track down this one!" She pointed at Lionel. "And he didn't even smell it on me!"

Sterling crossed his arms, "I think I speak for all of us when I say that your imitation is not flattery."

"The constabulary will require a perpetrator," added Gil.

"I thought the bloodshed had been me," defended Lionel.

"Well, it wasn't!" Denise produced her infamous hunting knife and waved it. "Be careful, I'm good with this." She dove at Brian and went snicker-snack multiple times.

Brian forlornly watched his suit fall to pieces at his feet, "So much wasted effort".

Igor stepped forward, "This is very inappropriate, young lady."

Mira placed a steadying hand on Gil, "Remember how it's all right to agree to disagree."

Sterling made a grab for Denise, but she dodged and slashed and darted and sliced.

Two more new suits hung in tatters.

Denise leaned back from the Monster, the Lab Assistant, and the Zombie, all of whom looked intensely annoyed. Her shoulder blades brushed a thick body emitting a fish aroma.

Gil placed a hand on either side of Denise's head and twisted.

Lionel screamed, though Farrah quickly enveloped him in linen.

MOST OF THE EVIL

Igor waved his arm for Brian to stay with him. Not known for their ambulatory skills, zombies tended to lag. "This is Tyler," Igor introduced Brian to the young man in the cage.

Tyler dragged himself along the floor and begged, "You need to tell my family where I am." Then he saw Brian and realized the futility of asking anything of yet another monster.

Igor had already moved further into his custom basement. "Come along."

Brian ignored the vocal victim. Most of the wall space contained various workplaces, glistening with cleanliness. "You have done something special down here."

Igor shared his crooked grin. "I appreciate the compliment from a friend and peer. You're one of the few visitors who leaves with a functioning cerebral cortex."

Brain smiled lopsidedly at the praise. "Not entirely functioning. Am a zombie."

"You undersell yourself, which is why I want to introduce you to..." Igor moved quickly to the distant corner and turned on an overhead light. A thick glass barrier surrounded a large cell. Inside, a man in a track suit sat on a recliner. "This is Dr. Liebermensch."

The doctor levered himself to his feet and strolled to the barrier. "Igor, you must let me go. What did you intend by bringing me here..."

"Sh, shh, shhh, and I'll explain. This is my friend, Brian, and he has been reading self-help books," said Igor.

"In and of itself, not a problem...," said Liebermensch.

Brian approached, "I suffer from a Negation Delirium."

Liebermensch nodded, "Yes, le délire des négations. Traditionally, it is Cotard's syndrome." He motioned behind Brian. "Please sit."

"I have a syndrome?" Brian settled onto a ratty sofa, raising a cloud of dust. "I appreciate you seeing me on short notice."

"I would suggest it is the heavy-handedness rather than the urgency which concerns me." The doctor encompassed his cell. His face remained blank. "Igor briefed me a little."

Brian raised a hand, about to speak, but then collapsed in on himself. On his third try, he managed, "I have broken adrift. And I talk to anyone. I managed to make an appointment with this one doctor finally. He listened to me pretty well. As I left, he poked me in the ribs while declaring I suffered from Negation Delirium. I surprised him when his finger went right into my ribcage."

Liebermensch rolled his fingers. "You believe you are a zombie."

"You've met Igor," responded Brian. "Is it so hard to believe?"

"I have met Igor. If I'm being entirely honest, Brian, friends like Igor might well inspire depression, hypochondria, or even somatoparaphrenia." Liebermensch pointed to the gleaming metal surfaces across the basement. "This place is a den of doom. You need to go outside and see the sun. You need to go where people spend their time living instead of obsessed with death."

"All right, Doc, but isn't one of the symptoms for a Negation Delirium to believe part of your body is decaying?" Brian rose to his feet in another haze of dust. Shambling forward, he stood by the airholes in the plexiglass. "Look at this and tell me I'm deluded." Brian rolled up a sleeve to reveal unskinned muscle lined with black vessels and dried sheaths. "This looks bad to me. Take a sniff." He looked at the still seated doctor. "I'm not playing around, Doc. Come over here and have a good inhale." Brian pressed the rottenest piece of his arm over the cut circles in the wall.

Liebermensch wavered between several types of surrender. He could admit his powerlessness or he could accept inevitable not-too-distant death. Pushed upright by the desire to live, he walked unsteadily to Brian's arm. He staggered with the first sniff.

"Is this what Negation Delirium smells like?" asked Brian.

"It's hardly a delirium if our mutual reason acknowledges the decay as fact." Liebermensch fell back out of odor range. "You require urgent medical care."

"But I'm already dead."

"You can't be." Liebermensch buried his nose in the crook of his elbow and coughed.

Brian opened his shirt, revealing an exposed cavity. "I'm better than the visible man. I bet you wish you had me to study while in medical school."

Liebermensch wandered back to his chair and carefully lowered himself. Emotion finally crossed his face, as of a man calculating his chances. He may have discovered a way forward. "Perhaps we can assist one another? We could meet for daily sessions, even twice per day."

"Doc, you look fragile." Brian turned to go. "Let me talk with Igor. He might have had another use for you in mind."

Brian had to cross the basement to reach the stairs. Almost there, a hand touched Brian's ankle. Looking down, he saw Tyler scrambling back from the front of his cage.

"I'm sorry, I'm sorry," pleaded the desperate young man.

"Igor does not trade in the good people of the world," said Brian. "You will be even more sorry."

"Can you do one thing for me?" Tyler's voice reached a new pitch. "Please, please." When Brian did not turn away, Tyler plunged ahead. "The monster has magic markers over on his whiteboard. Could you bring me one, a permanent one? Please?"

Brian shrugged and did as asked. He watched as Tyler popped the lid off the marker and wrote on his limbs.

"What are you doing?" asked Brian.

"I'm putting my name and phone number on all the parts the monster is going to cut off. The Amputator has been doing this for a couple years. The cops haven't caught him, but everyone has read about him."

"This Amputator? He cuts off limbs?" Brian glanced at the nearby circular saw.

Tyler studied the genitals between his legs. He stretched and manipulated until he had a satisfactory writing surface and scribbled away. "He scatters them all over the tri-county area." Tyler froze. "He's coming!"

Igor arrived at the foot of the stairs.

"Are you the Amputator?" asked Brian.

"No, I am not," answered Igor with an annoyed look at Tyler. "Whoever it is should be called the Abomination. He is a disaster with the surgical saw and no respect for the families left behind."

"There. Feel better?" Brian asked Tyler.

"No, I don't!" said Tyler to their backs as they went upstairs. "Then what am I doing here?!"

Returning, Igor crouched like a baseball catcher, forcing his massive thigh muscles to press against his pants so they shined. "I like to keep my hand in." The Mad Scientist's Assistant studied Tyler and his cage. "What would you do if I set you free?"

Tyler stopped in mid-scribble. The black and blue around his eyes highlighted their minute shift between the two monsters standing beyond his bars. He scuttled precisely to Igor. As he spoke, he offered the marker to Igor. "I would ask if you needed to hold something of mine as collateral for my promise never to speak of this."

Brian laid a hand on Igor's shoulder. "I thought we agreed we don't play with our food."

Through a vigorous forearm muscle spasm, Tyler maintained eye contact with Igor.

Igor used Brian's body to pull himself upright. As they walked away, he loudly said, "This one makes me come apart at the seams."

As the door at the top of the stairs creaked, Tyler's voice went hoarse as he asked, "Do we have a deal?"

***

"What is this?" asked Brian, holding up the bourbon glass. When he shifted, the plastic between him and the seat cushion crackled.

Igor recently upgraded his family room to a sitting parlor with oversized chairs for his only guests. The plastic protectors came out for certain friends. "One of my former employers, Doctor de Selby, would spend too much time at his club in London. He would stumble home drunk late at night, I would help his butler carry him to his bedroom. Then I would stand outside his door eavesdropping as he would ramble on about the joys of his leisure time. Truly, he was a failure in the laboratory, but I have always carried the images he conjured in his delirium."

Brian nodded politely. "But this beverage? It delights me, which I haven't been able to say since my first taste of brains. They provided a marvelous mouth sensation and this is different, but... I don't remember joy..." He leaned back into the cushions until the furniture creaked.

"I distilled the lymphatic fluid of a young woman who tried to steal packages off my front porch," explained Igor.

"The still I saw in the corner of the basement?" checked Brian.

"Hardly," Igor raised his hand in refutation. "Those are brine buckets. I've already started my pickling for Thanksgiving."

"More of the incompetent thief?" Brian sipped.

"I had planned to add most of Tyler downstairs, but now I think of him by name."

"You can't identify the ones you intend to eat," agreed Brian. "I can hardly pursue anyone if I can call them by name." He stood and studied the portrait on the wall. "Someone added Gil." A strip of canvas had been tacked to the painting. "I seem to be the only one missing."

After a few contemplative moments, Igor asked, "Are we become moot, bumbling, and pointless?"

"Not if you keep brewing up potions as wonderful as this," Brian raised his glass to his host.

"Hear, hear," agreed Igor.

They basked in the glow of the drink and their companionship until Brian tugged at an exposed tendon in his wrist.

"You are disturbed?" asked Igor. "I can't keep repairing you."

"I'm not a fast thinker," advanced Brian, "but you know more about the doctor and the naked man in the basement than you have said."

Igor's grin looked like a cemetery under a full moon. "You sell yourself short. You have discerned what has stumped the constabulary for miles around. Dr. Liebermensch is in fact the Amputator. He acquired hapless Tyler before I obtained the pair of them."

***

"I used to read books," said Brian, once again seated before Dr. Liebermensch. "I don't remember anyone mentioning zombies. The vampires had Dracula and the werewolves..."

"In reality," the Doctor took his throne when he saw the zombie approaching, "many of your designated monsters are concepts conjured by an oral tradition. Cultures summon necessary anthropomorphic horrors to elucidate the unexplainable."

Brian had located a worn out easy chair in a basement corner and covered it with a dusty afghan. His hands twisted the knitted yarn into a clump. When he tried to undo the bundle, his finger bones and string bits grew entangled. Refusing to raise his eyes from the mess, Brian quietly stewed.

"You used to read, you say?" inquired Liebermensch.

Brian ground his teeth until one popped loose and rattled to the basement floor. "I watched movies at the drive-in. I drove a car. I had an A in pre-calculus. I took a year off before college to raise money to pay for it. I spent all my spare time reading. I wanted to be..."

Liebermensch waited patiently, but finally asked, "What, pray tell?"

"Nothing," said Brian. Slowly at first, but accelerating, Brian unraveled his bindings. He backed away from the chair and blanket before returning his attention to the doctor. "I can't remember when I last dreamed of being anything other than what I am right now."

Liebermensch shrugged disinterested approval, "You have accomplished your dreams."

"You don't understand." Brian squared up to the see-through cage. "What about you? Do you have dreams?"

"Every person alive does," answered Liebermensch. "For me, I am interested in humanity, in what makes people tick. Naturally, visions originate in the mind, but my interest extends far beyond, from the chemistry to the engineering of the human body."

"You should have met Igor under different circumstances," commented Brian. "We have this other friend who... never mind."

With three steps, Liebermensch stood by the interior edge of his cell, "How dare you consider yourself worthy of talking to me as an equal? Do you summon the cosmos?" Through an airhole, Liebermensch wagged a finger at the zombie.

Brian leapt forward and bit off the top two knuckles of Liebermensch's right index finger before heading for the stairs.

Behind him, Liebermensch opined through a tight jaw, "Don't believe the hype, Brian. You do not behave like a monster in order to affirm your existence—no exercise in validation for you when masticating the flesh of a homo sapiens. You manifest in flesh..." A long pause followed.

Turning a corner, Brian glanced back. The doctor licked the bloody stump of his finger and then sucked the leaking wound. The zombie halted in a puddle of shadow and pulled his shirt up, displaying his torso. Large swathes of missing flesh revealed brown and purple muscle. His exposed intestines coiled like an emergency firehose unused for decades in a closed public school.

Brian spat out the doctor's finger. Then he retrieved the masticated digit. Adjusting his grip, he wiggled the tip of the detached finger across his belly. Long ago, Brian had been told a person could not tickle themselves. His undead chuckle sounded like the cracking of a vinyl record, sun-desiccated on the front seat of a Chevy Corvair.

Brian stopped with the tickling. He nibbled the finger until he reached the foot of the basement stairs. He raised a pausing hand to Tyler who took the hint. "Hey, Igor!"

Heavy footsteps pounded above them and the basement door flew open. "Yes?"

"My thing might be metaphors!" announced Brian. "Like a once leaky faucet, I've been plumber-adjusted to my proper functioning!"

Tyler and Igor (and possibly Liebermensch) all took the opportunity to tell Brian he had used a simile. The basement door closed again, causing Tyler to sag.

Brian lowered his hand and spoke to Tyler, "I may have a way we can help one another." Before Tyler could respond, Brian headed into the aisles of Igor's basement hoarding.

"I am the archaeologist of my friend's life," stated Brian, enjoying the taste of the words. He shifted boxes and looked under tables. By an amazingly shiny boiler system, Brian found a gun safe. With a sigh, Brian passed Tyler and climbed the steps. He found the key hanging by the basement light switch.

Nodding to Tyler as he passed him once again, Brian said, "I am the world's foremost forgetful alpinist."

Tyler grabbed through his bars for the key.

"Wait," Brian raised a finger, not his own, and tossed Liebermensch's loose finger into Tyler's cage. "I have something better for you."

Tyler crouched over the nubbin on the floor of his cage and studied it. He had so many questions, but he maintained his aural focus on those receding steps. Brian's behavior felt important. The Zombie walked like an old man in oversized sandals. The pace sounded determined with the occasional break for contemplation.

In the distance, metal hinges opened.

The prisoner at the other end of the basement cried out, "I am going to bill you for all these hours! Your insurance won't cover you for most of them, especially when I tell them how you consistently miss appointments!"

A clatter like a high school locker falling over echoed toward Tyler.

Brian turned into view and grew larger with his approach. "I carry your freedom," announced the zombie. At a yard's distance, he proffered a handgun, "How is this as a metaphor?"

For his entire life, Tyker never understood the saying about waiting for the other shoe to drop. Did they mean someone wore the shoes and you anticipated their footfalls? Did people hang their shoes on hooks back in the day? In this moment, crouching over a masticated finger, in a cage in a basement, so exhausted his terror felt like an emotion he could examine at a distance, Tyler tensed with anticipation. "It's a good metaphor," he said to Brian.

"You have met Dr. Liebermensch?" asked Brian.

Tyler sensed the brain fog returning. "My psychiatrist? Are the cops here? I told you before..."

Brian shook his head. Even with missing parts from his face, he oozed pity. "Liebermensch is the reason you're here. He wanted to kill you and my friend saved your life."

Tyler swept the finger across the floor and out of his cage, bringing the present into high definition. He had the slimmest of control over the current moment. "Your friend?"

"Liebermensch is the guy who amputates. He wants to understand how you work," explained Brian.

"The last thing I remember," Tyler pulled at his memories in order to undo the tightly wrapped bundle of his life before this basement. "I had an appointment with this psychiatrist. I saw him because I had suspicions... I had lost someone close to me. They had been... cut apart." Tyler pulled back into the present. "I told him I had a fear of flying."

The only sound in the basement became the inhaling and exhaling of its occupants.

Tyler looked at Brian for the first time and realized how much worse a zombie appeared up close. "Fear of flying looks pretty fucking ridiculous right now, I have to tell you."

With deliberation, Brian nodded. "If I give you this gun, will you go over and shoot Liebermensch dead?"

"Why me?" asked Tyler, immediately regretting the response.

"You've earned the right."

"What are you going to do to me after I kill him?" asked Tyler.

Brian looked toward the imprisoned doctor and then listened above. "Let you go up the stairs, I suppose."

Tyler mimicked Brian's scanning pattern before answering, "Give it here."

The gun almost reached Tyler's hand before Brian pulled it back. He looked hard into the eyes of the naked young man. "We're not the monsters. Liebermensch is." Brian undid the lock and shuffled back.

Stepping into freedom, Tyler accepted the gun. He tested its heft in his hand. He pointed it at Brian. "Back up a little further. I'm going to leave now."

"Really?" Fully perplexed, Brian did not immediately process the command.

"I said to back the hell up!" Tyler's voice had grown dusty, but he projected.

The extending silence broke when Liebermensch called, "What's going on? That sounded like a breakout! Don't leave me!"

The basement door opened and Igor descended the stairs. Before reaching the bottom, he inquired, "What have you done, Brian?"

"Stop right there!" ordered Tyler.

"You would like to leave?" said Igor. "By all means, you'll find egress in the kitchen at the top of the steps." Igor sidestepped allowing Tyler access to the exit. "Please bear in mind my sole intention had been to stop Liebermensch's predations as the Amputator."

Focused on departure, Tyler backed up the stairwell halfway before turning and running. A stumble, a door bang, a knocked over chair, commotion in the kitchen, and Tyler departed the house.

"I made a mistake," confessed Brian.

"You grow more innocent as time passes. Others might find it charming, but I miscalculated because of it. It's difficult not to look at you and see a monster, even for me." Igor headed up to the kitchen. "Let's discuss our options."

Instead of talking, they closed the open door into the backyard. They straightened the furniture. Tyler had left the gun on the counter beside the sink. Also, he had left the vicinity.

Later, standing in the kitchen, Igor handed the gun to Brian. "I salute your plan, but we no longer have a likely suspect for the police to pursue. Still, someone needs to eliminate the evil Liebermensch."

***

Igor and Brian drove the mad psychiatrist's body to the Amputator's storage unit where they deposited the bullet-riddled corpse and the murder weapon. A blood stain in the hallway and a jimmied lock ought to attract enough attention.

Igor had extracted Tyler from the storage facility in the first place. The addition of the handgun with a partial print or two ought to lead the investigation to Tyler as the heroic escapee who put an end to the Amputator's protracted line of limbs.

By the time the Zombie and the All-Purpose Science Ogre returned to Igor's, the discreet moving company had loaded a truck with the contents of the above ground floors. Their special division worked under Igor's personal direction for the remaining possessions of his home.

As Igor and Brian drove after the departing movers, Igor pressed the radio button which would initiate a gas main explosion beneath his former home.

Settled in a new abode later, when he unpacked the group portrait of his makeshift family, Igor found a photo-booth strip of Brian tacked to the canvas.

I Measure My Life Out With Coffee Spoons

Igor walked into the kitchen and stopped. Row after row of spotless pots and pans hung from ceiling racks. A walk-in fireplace dominated the opposite wall. A lone coffee cup bearing a spoon sat beside a stainless steel sink.

"Glorious, isn't it?" asked Mira, coming up behind him.

"I had no idea. I've never seen any galley like it." Igor took two steps forward and stopped. Eyeing the appliances lined up to his right and to his left, he had no idea where to turn. "You could prepare a feast for four thousand here."

"You have an accurate eye," nodded Mira.

"Mad scientists tend to punish severely. It pays to have good eyes, even if you acquire them from an unwilling donor." Igor vacillated. "But you don't cook."

"I like the smells," said Mira. "They generate memories. Vlad would host large parties. He invited anyone and everyone and fed them all. Talk about glorious." She brushed Igor's collar. "You would have loved the lawn games." She opened the nearest huge refrigerator, revealing a single jar of olives, which she placed on a countertop. Opening a drawer, she located a canister of toothpicks.

"How do you keep track of where everything is?" asked the former Assistant to Insane Investigators.

"My minions are extremely detail oriented."

"Still," wondered Igor.

The Vampire made the olive jar pop. Her thin fingers proffered a red-black oval. "Vlad had a way with people." Her other hand skewered the fruit from bottom to top. She pushed the olive toward Igor until he opened his mouth. The toothpick crunched as he chewed. "Like you, my dear." Mira sniffed the air. "You always find your way to the basement where my less accurate minions wind up."

Igor extracted a bundle from his pants pocket and placed it on a prep table. "Kidneys." He peeled the plastic wrap and wax paper back to reveal two fresh pieces of meat, slightly bloody.

Mira slipped a finger across the organs and tasted a drop from each. "Paulo won't survive without either kidney."

"I made assumptions about your intentions regarding Paulo," said Igor. "Now I feel bad for not asking him his name."

"He should have introduced himself." Mira studied the kidneys. "You could have selected any part of the body."

"At the start of certain days, I appreciate the tang of urine."

"You are an unusual man, dear Igor," said Mira.

***

People-watching, Brian the Zombie sat on a bench in downtown Sioux City. The sun had set an hour previously and his sort of crowd had emerged. Brian had a fondness for outsiders ever since he had stepped back among the living.

For once, he did not feel hungry, probably due to the vacuum salesperson he had eaten mid-morning. Brian leaned back and closed his eyes. On a full stomach, he could ignore his own scent and enjoy the sounds of the world. Sandals and sneakers and dress shoes and high heels all passed on the sidewalk. Car engines rumbled reassuringly. He could imagine himself back in the world, fully fleshed and totally invested.

A dark purring entered Brian's ear canal. His eyelids parted as he followed the action. The pursuit happened in a nearby alley. The cat with the bright white paws stalked her prey as silently as a buried coffin.

"I thought I'd lost you," muttered Brian. Pretending to be unaware, he reached into his backpack and extracted an old John Saul paperback. After flipping pages for a moment, Brian surrendered to the inevitable.

Swinging the pack over his shoulder, Brian shuffled to the dark alley where the cat sounds originated. He found the feline sitting on its haunches, holding a mouse like an ice cream cone. The feline tongue darted out and licked the exposed brain.

As Brian observed the situation, the rodent managed a pathetic squeak of inquiry, "What fresh hell be this?" perhaps.

The human Zombie leaned against a convenient dumpster. "You don't seem to understand," he said to the cat. "We do not travel together. The movies might make you believe we travel in great devouring herds, but we're basically out for ourselves."

Brian shifted his pack and extracted a Tupperware container. "It's a little weird how much more satisfaction I get out of making this plastic lid burp than I did when alive."

The cat licked twice and then studied Brian. The contents of Brian's food container interested its undead mind terribly.

Brian scooped out a strand of brain and ate it. "I may not travel in a herd, but I do have friends. They mostly treat me like Joey from that TV show- a little slow, but likable. Only Igor understands what I can be if I'm well fed." Brian shook his pack which emitted the sounds of many brains in many containers. "How about you?" Brian crouched and placed the open container on the ground.

The cat immediately dropped the mouse and bounded over to Brian's feet. Giving him a glance to ensure his intentions, it tested the scent and then the taste of the offering. Satisfied, it tucked in.

The mouse with the missing skullcap stumbled out of the shadows with its nose high in the air. Ignored by the cat, the rodent approached the contained brain and extracted a handful of neurons.

"You made a friend, too," said Brian to the cat.

✳✳✳

Shortly after nightfall, Mira found Igor in the basement of her castle. "You ordered him a hospital bed? I heard the delivery truck."

Igor sat beside Paulo. "He lives!" He mixed frustration with confusion.

"Not only saw the movie," Mira nodded, "but it was I who suggested to James Whale that he give Mary's book a read."

Igor studied her placid face. "No one appreciates a name dropper."

Mira watched Igor eat off a plate in his lap. "Are you consuming more of my minions?"

"This is Paulo's liver," Igor dipped a cracker in a green mass. "Not as fatty as goose, but passable. If you allowed your workers to eat fast-food three times per week, then..."

Mira held up her hand, "I allow generous breaks. They decide how to spend their free time."

***

Standing in the alcove beside Mira, Farrah adjusted her linen wraps across her hips. "It's the long car ride that does it. Mummification was not designed for vinyl seats."

"I wanted to speak with you before we went downstairs," said Mira. "If anyone asks, I showed you my favorite painting."

Farrah studied the canvas on the wall. "I don't recall a pyramid of skulls from Cézanne's official catalog."

"Come now, dear," said the Countess, "you must have a few items which have bypassed official recognition."

Farrah extracted a magnifying glass from her person and examined the painted surface. "These are modern materials. Cézanne has been dead for over a century."

Mira shrugged, "Which doesn't mean he had to stop painting."

"You didn't," concern colored Farrah's tone. "It's one thing to collect the art, but entirely another to collect the artist." Her eyes shifted down, left, and right. "He is not sequestered in the basement, is he?"

"As a matter of fact, he's designing sets for a small ballet company in Paris."

"It's unfair to the living."

Mira tittered until the Mummy joined in. Mice peering through a hole in the corner ran away in terror.

Eventually settling down, Farrah secreted the eyeglass and said, "Very well. Send Cézanne to my place outside of Cairo. I would love to see if he can do for an archaeological site what he did for quarries." She turned her back to the bruised purple and cadmium yellow, "Tell me about Igor."

The vampire's sigh sounded like a cracked bone flute. "He merely sits there beside the dead man, as if waiting for something."

"He has worked with corpses before."

Mira reached behind Farrah and slid a shutter over the painting. "You need to observe the reality."

***

The cat and the mouse finished Brian's snack container. The mouse plummeted onto its backside, grinning like a mammal on an endorphin high. The cat turned away from Brian and raised its tail high. Sashaying down the alley, it beckoned.

However, the feline promenaded only ten yards when a tomcat dropped into its path. The stranger hissed, causing both cats to stretch vertically and call out in angry exhalations. They stepped sideways and back the other way, like two determined people confronting a doorway from opposite sides.

The alley cat pressed forward. It leapt and grabbed the other's head. Both howled, though only the domesticated one did so because of pain.

The commotion triggered a response in the rodent brain at Brian's feet. The mouse staggered upright, studied the fighting felines, and headed into the fray, gaining speed with every step. It appeared ready to dive straight into the zombie cat's very visible anus, but instead cleared the back of the cat by six inches. Arriving teeth first on the tomcat's nose, it bit hard, and peeled a strip of flesh from nostril to eyebrow.

The alley denizen reared back in agony. The mouse dangled off the side of its face. Shaken vigorously, the mouse traced an arc in the air, using cat flesh like a kite tail. The undead rodent rolled until coming to rest in front of Brian.

The zombie cat took the opportunity to pounce and claw the alley cat into submission. The poor animal withheld any outcries, unwilling to attract an animal which would prey upon its injuries. Little did it suspect it would receive no respite.

Brian closed his eyes and thought about the times he had lost himself in undead rage. The black curtain fell. Later, you faced so much blood and so many obligations.

Fur brushed against his ankles. Brian watched the deadly mouse and cat amble like old comrades to the sidewalk at the alley opening.

Back the other way, an awful thing struggled to place its legs underneath its body. The alley cat had risen. Brian walked slowly to the newly undead. The poor creature had one eye left. Its throat bled. Its tongue protruded from a cheek hole.

Brian stomped on its skull before it could be fully reborn.

***

Escorted by the Countess, Farrah stopped at the foot of the cavern stairs. Mira undersold the size of her basement, even if it lay beneath a castle transported from the old country to the Hudson Valley. Money had never been an obstacle for either of them, but Farrah, daughter of the pyramids, had spent her last few lifetimes avoiding anything ostentatious.

Aboveground, Mira's visible abode spoke of her longing for the old country. Down here, Mira maintained the interests she had cultivated across five centuries. Within sight, the subterranean chambers contained a warehouse, working surgery, modern laboratory, recording studio, and carpentry workshop.

A dozen yards away, Igor sat beside a hospital bed occupied by a sleeping young man.

Farrah looked at Mira, "You said the man had died."

"As soon as a person chooses to enter my employ, they depart the world of the living," Mira vocally shrugged, long ago deciding the physical gesture was vulgar. "What do you do with your minions?"

"We had slaves when I spent my youth beside the Nile, but I have never claimed followers since."

"Slaves?" Mira commented.

Farrah approached Igor and stood on the other side of the bed. "Hello."

"I expected her to call Sterling," said Igor.

***

Preceded by a young man, Mira descended the basement stairs. "I have identified a donor for you, Igor. Meet Kepler Morgenstern. I found him outside a bar."

Igor and Farrah stood on opposite sides of the hospital bed. The patient wore a muddy yellow hue.

"You're both awfully quiet. Don't tell me poor Norman has died." Mira gripped Kepler's bicep as the prospective donor turned back to the stairs.

"No, he lives," Farrah said. "Do you notice, Mira, how difficult it can be at times to talk undead to living? Even as friends? Their obsessions can be exhausting, don't you find?"

Igor ignored the Mummy. "Is Kepler the right blood type?"

Mira stared at Igor before saying slowly, "In my humble opinion, yes. Also, he served as the designated driver for the night. His kidneys should be flush with healthy color."

Igor nodded, "Who wants to assist?"

Farrah and Mira headed for the steps while Kepler fainted.

***

"I'm sorry it took me so long to arrive," said Sterling.

"You walked," said Mira.

"I walked," agreed the Monster. He studied the heavy boots which he never removed, even when they annoyed his host. No one needed to see his conglomerated feet. "Tell me about the painting."

"It's a pyramid of skulls by Paul Cézanne."

"No shit," agreed Sterling. "I spend a lot of time outdoors, but it doesn't mean I've never been to a museum. I've probably been in more art galleries than you."

Mira raised her arms and pointed at herself in that do-you-realize-who-you're-talking-to gesture which she might have invented.

"Fine." Sterling resisted the urge to challenge his second oldest friend. "I have just come off the road." The Monster's oldest friend sat in the castle basement. "The colors are upsetting. Can you cover it up again?"

Mira did as the Simulacrum asked, but then she did not leave the small viewing room. The air grew damp and smelled of boot mud. "Igor arrived two weeks ago, too quiet and extraordinarily distracted."

"I saw him four months ago. During our visit, he mentioned how the vet had described a deadly disease which could afflict his cat."

"He mentioned nothing." Mira sniffled. "I'm allergic, so it's just as well he didn't bring the nasty beast."

"It might explain his mood," said Sterling.

"He's been dismantling my help," complained Mira.

"You drain them when they outlive their usefulness."

"I'm not a charity," agreed the Countess, not shrugging.

"You survive on the backs of the proletariat. On their blood and sweat."

Mira nodded, "Though mostly their blood."

Sterling nodded and they both had a good chuckle.

"You're more and more of a Trotskyite with each passing decade," said Mira.

"I ought to see him now," insisted Sterling.

Mira shrugged. Then frowned with self-disgust.

***

Sterling whispered to Mira, "Good God, how much of your staff has he dissipated?" They stood a few yards back from Igor and a young man on a hospital bed.

"Counting this boy, three," said Mira.

"You made it sound like he had devastated your entire operation," responded Sterling.

"Three more have run off and two have refused to set foot anywhere near Igor, who they assume could appear anywhere. They have barricaded themselves in the wine cellar."

"It must be terrible for you," sympathized Sterling.

"Not really. I use the secret passage."

"The people hiding there are right to be afraid," said Sterling.

"No one who works for me is ever wrong to be afraid," stated Mira.

"What is the lad's name?"

"Cooper," said Mira.

"That's a job, not a name." Sterling crossed his arms.

"Should he be a Taylor?"

Sterling left Mira where she stood. His approach across the concrete floor sounded like the repeated dropping of a rubber bowling ball. Igor did not look up and Cooper appeared unable to do so. Sterling stood beside the man who had assisted the man who gave him life. A sensation passed between them and Sterling placed an arm across Igor's broad shoulders. "What's with all the silverware?" Sterling asked gently. He pointed at a nearby medical tray leavened with cutlery of singular purpose.

"Have you ever counted the minutes in a single human life?" Igor spoke softly, gently caressing the leg of his patient. "It's well over a half million. Isn't the number staggering?" He reached for a spoon from the pile and held it up to the light. "This is designed for consuming grapefruit."

Sterling stepped around the bed so he could better see his friend's face. "I've never given it much thought, but I understand it is not such a large number in years."

"Help me turn him on his side," requested Igor.

Once they had Mira's stirring, terrified minion in place, Sterling could see a gaping hole in the man's lower back. A viscous liquid leaked from the wound. Igor inserted the spoon and twisted. The patient cried out. Igor offered a spoonful of unidentifiable organ to Sterling. "See if you can classify it by taste."

Sterling insisted they lay the poor man on his belly. Then the Monster produced a pocket square with which he wiped the man's tears. Only then did Sterling accept the morsel. "Spleen? No, no. Is it bladder? It's rather bland."

"There's wine on the table," suggested Igor, pointing with the spoon.

Sterling went through a whole routine with his first drink, sniffing, examining, mouth rinsing, and finally drinking. "It's outstanding for New Zealand."

"Mira wouldn't open the cellars in the sub-basement to me. She fears I'm depressed and I would squander anything special on tastebuds which are emotionally anesthetized." After a pause, Igor added, "She's probably right." He took a coffee carafe off the table and filled a well-used cup. Adding powdered creamer with a spoon from the mound on the tray, he stirred meditatively. "I haven't been sleeping well."

"You wrote me how Socks died." Sterling scanned the near-by walls. He wondered how much Mira had spent transporting the old stones from her native country. Knowing her, the entire foundation rested on a shipload of Transylvanian soil. "A long time ago, I met a little girl who befriended me. With experience, I can see how we each thought of the other as a pet. When she drowned, I struggled to make sense of my emotions."

"I have watched hundreds of subjects die," Igor encompassed the man on the bed with his spoon. "I have fulfilled shopping lists to the detriment of living donors."

"All I am saying," insisted the Monster, "is you do not need to measure your life by spoonfuls of sugar."

Igor stuck out a gray tongue and licked his stirring utensil. "Brian stayed with me."

Sterling dragged a nearby recliner across the floor before carrying it the last few feet. He sat and adjusted his limbs to fit as comfortably as possible. "I suspect Brian is bipolar."

"No," said Igor, "he simply has hunger issues."

A familiar voice shouted down the stairs, "Knock! Knock!"

"Oh, God," said Sterling.

"He's all right," said Igor softly.

Lionel descended into view, "I didn't want to interrupt anything." He came near but stopped when he saw the bed and the sundry accoutrements of Igor's activities. "I see you're busy..."

Igor beckoned him closer, "Finishing up."

"For a werewolf, you are exceptionally squeamish," commented Sterling.

Lionel tilted his head at the Monster and narrowed his eyes.

"You forget our friend is not entirely conscious during his nightly forays," said Igor.

"There is a difference between what I do to survive and what you do as a hobby," said Lionel.

Sterling laughed, "I consider my actions above such dissembling. Here, try the wine. Did you see Mira?"

***

Igor could not sleep.

For the sake of the mad scientists who traditionally employed him, he had remained awake for days. Usually, they provided pep pills or electric shocks to stimulate him. His subsequent erratic behavior went unnoticed since the bonker boffins consumed uppers by the handful, growing prone to outrageous outcries and anticlimactic accidents.

Whenever Igor closed his eyes, the bad thoughts returned: listening to the veterinarian tell him about chronic kidney disease in cats. Socks, not currently diagnosed with the ailment, sat on the examining table, no different than he had been for every other appointment. The solution appeared obvious to Igor. He would perform a transplant.

As he relived the disastrous surgery, Igor could never decide whether to force his eyes to open or to squeeze even tighter. He had sewn his eyelids shut one nightmare-filled night in a Motel 6. They tore open the next afternoon when he tripped over a lamp cord.

He had done nothing wrong- merely wanted to improve his pet. The veterinarian had recommendations for prevention of future problems. Igor preferred drastic action now. He had spent centuries in drafty laboratories working with men of incomparable vision. They had always been willing to do the unthinkable in service of the unbelievable.

As a thirteen year old, Igor had replaced his finger because Luisa Van Trottenberg had told him it looked odd. He had altered his hairline, left ear, and buttocks before he had finished growing. The latter operation may have caused his stooped stature. It proved exceptionally difficult to sculpt one's rear end from the front side without assistance. Still, the result had been good enough to obtain Igor his first position as a laboratory assistant. Crazy Camilla the Lady Chemist of Kent would pinch Igor's bottom for good luck before pouring her latest concoction down the gullet of an unfortunate.

Sadly, Igor had been wrong about cats. And he had been wrong about death. In his worst moments, Igor watched a long progression of experimental subjects die. The last, his small, happy cat, paused while the black parade moved off into the distance, as if the whiskered face longed to stay.

What did this say about all those laboratories and all those mad scientists?

What did it say about Igor?

For decades he had spectacularly delayed the inevitable.

Igor had never pondered inevitable death or the afterlife. From his vantage, it appeared to be a choice made by so many ignorant, lazy people seeking comfort. He could not say the same for his lovely feline, Socks.

The slightest hint of spirituality could be the death knell for an immortal.

Gil stepped out of the shadows. "Mira has been dead. She is every day and then comes back. I could be wrong. Perhaps you should talk to her." The fish man saw the question on Igor's face. "You talk in your sleep. It sounded like a crisis of faith. I've spent time in churches. How does anyone walk the Earth for this long without occasionally hoping for answers?"

"Have you found any?" Igor shook a nearby wine bottle to confirm its emptiness.

"Being inside the church gave me the peace to leave the church. I'm grateful it's there, but life can't be contained by any philosophy." Touching assorted items, Gil walked through Igor's work area.

Igor may or may not have heard. He had wandered off.

Gil took a seat and looked at the patient in the bed.

After a few minutes, Igor returned with a pair of bottles from Mira's cellar. "Drink with me." He poured them each a glass. "What are you doing here?"

"Mira reached out. She wants you to leave," answered Gil.

Igor paused in mid-drink. "Did you kill poor young Cooper?"

"What you were doing- it was an unkindness," the Creature explained.

"I agree," said Igor. "I can't abide meddling though."

"I stopped the boy's pain." Gil's eyes displayed all pupil. They reflected the ceiling light behind Igor. "Do you want me to do the same for you?"

Igor went to a chair and settled heavily into it. "I am not chasing death."

Gil waited because Igor looked like he would continue. When nothing came forth, the Fish Man dragged a chair closer to his friend and sat. "Then what are you doing here?"

"I understood my purpose," explained Igor. "And then I became a cat owner." Igor wiped a tear. "Haven't you ever wondered why you're here?"

"I'm here because Mira can be a royal pain in the ass if you ignore her."

"I don't mean here-here. I mean the big here." The cellar grew quiet. Igor listened to their respiration and wondered about their anatomical differences. Gil sounded like he contained a bubble producing machine, although heavily muted. The Fish Man's gaze always focused somewhere over your shoulder. "I left Brian with Socks, because I could not stay after what I had done. Mira has allowed me to see how close the living can come to death before returning to life."

"What have you discovered?" asked Gil.

"Socks has likely died in my absence." Igor longed to bathe in darkness and silence.

"We weren't designed for these sorts of questions," said Gil eventually. "We're supposed to be nightmare fodder. Existential terror becomes self-destructive for people who want to instigate specific fears. We are the latter and should avoid dwelling on the former. I never understood this particular worry."

"No one ever expected us to survive so long," expelled Igor.

"You need to cultivate more useful coping methods," said Gil.

"Did I mention how I measure my life in coffee spoons?" responded Igor.

Gil always stared back blankly, but this time he meant it.

"Maybe it wasn't you," said Igor.

Dust fell from overhead as heavy footsteps resounded through the dense stones between the first floor and cellar. Gil brushed the effluvia off his sleeves. He looked at Igor and they agreed, "Brian."

"I hope he locked the front door of my home like I asked," said Igor.

Before Gil could inquire, Brian pounded down the stairs. With arm extended, the Zombie walked to them and placed a set of keys in Igor's hand.

"You could have left them under the backdoor mat," said Igor.

Brian grunted. "You left me behind. I sympathize with depression, so I am not giving you a tough time, but maybe you should have checked on Socks one more time."

Tentative, awkward, tiny footpads sounded near the top of the stairs.

"Your cat," continued Brian, "bit me." He waved a hand at Igor. The gray pallor betrayed no wound. "Trust me. He received his piece of flesh. Sometimes I heal. You should look into why. I'd really like an explanation."

"I am a scientist's assistant, not a true mad doctor," said Igor.

"You've been operating without supervision for as long as I've known you," countered Gil. "As for you," the Fish Man turned on the Zombie, "we agreed not to reproduce."

"It's more difficult for Brian and Lionel," said Igor, distracted by his pet cat slowly descending the steps.

"I take care of my own culling," said Brian. "I made an executive decision and let this one live." He turned to look at Socks. "Neither of you thought I had any executive brain function left."

The cat sauntered to the trio, rubbing against each of their legs until recognizing something about Igor. He picked up the cat and cuddled it to his chest. His expressionless face held steady for only so long before he raised his gaze to the ceiling and sniffled.

Brian and Gil became interested in the surgical table beside Cooper's corpse.

Igor turned the bundle in his arms so he could study Socks' face. The feline raised a paw to Igor's nose and tapped once. A disturbing purr began deep within the cat torso. It sounded too loud and rattled like she had swallowed too many mouse bones.

Socks' belly burst open with a gash, revealing an extremely disturbed mouse. The rodent dropped to the floor. Socks twisted from Igor's grasp and leapt after its frenemy. Trailing two short intestinal strands, Socks chased after the stomach-juice-dripping, skullcap-deprived mouse.

All three Monsters stood terribly still and watched the eternal chase continue into the shadows.

"What do we do now?" asked Brian, eventually.

"How large is this cellar?" asked Gil.

"Quite large," answered Igor, "and this is the top level."

"What do we tell Mira?" asked Brian.

Gil wandered off for three minutes and returned with a bottle of wine. He arranged three comfortable chairs. Without a word, he poured three glasses. He beckoned them to sit with him. They tasted the wine.

"I don't know that we need to tell her anything," said Gil.

Disturbing The Dust

Lionel walked past the soda shop with only a glance at the cool malts and sodas on offer. The sun would set in an hour and the sidewalk still raised a heat shimmer as he strolled onto a side street. The tavern off Main Street attracted the college crowd because the proprietor had a willingness to be discreet. If you kept your behavior in check and kept paying for another drink, then you could stay.

The first time Lionel had entered Rockne's, the bartender had harassed him enough that Lionel had walked out. He returned the next night with his admission letter to Western Reserve Medical University dated 1957, a year earlier. Thus, Lionel demonstrated he was of age to drink and not the high school teenager he appeared to be. He did not elaborate how he had dropped out halfway through his first semester.

Lionel dressed dapper, sporting a Case University letter sweater which he had acquired from a wrestler who had died a year ago beneath Lionel's claws. Out here in the suburbs of Cleveland, people took a sweater at face value without inquiring into its provenance.

Two young women sat at the bar with an empty stool to their left. Most of the tables had been occupied by those dodging the heat. Lionel took the stool and eyed the book the woman next to him waved about.

"Is it a good read?" interrupted Lionel.

She turned on him with upraised tome. Her brown hair shifted about her face as she exhaled smoke to the side of his head. "Brenda bought it because her boyfriend talks all the time about Allen Ginsberg and she wants to be one up on him, so she bought this other book from the same guy who published **Howl**."

Lionel reached out to the book and held it still so he could read the cover. "Lawrence Ferlinghetti?"

"He's a poet," clarified Brenda from behind the book waver.

Lionel nodded over the shoulder of the intervening coed, who rolled her eyes and stubbed out her cigarette. He said, "I actually have a cousin who ran with the Beats. If he's the same Larry, then he could be a real hog at the dinner table."

Then the closer one extended her hand, "I'm Julianne." Her pulse twinkled under his touch. "Do you go to Case?"

Noting the bartender eavesdropping, Lionel smiled, "Used to, but now I spend my time at the medical school downtown."

"Really," Julianne touched the fabric of his sweater. "You must be awfully warm under there on a day like this. Or any day rolling around in those steamy wrestling rooms."

"Can I buy you and Brenda refreshers?" Lionel offered.

While they waited on their drinks, Julianne mentioned, "It's the summer solstice."

"A very poetic night, I hear," Lionel grinned and then hid his teeth. "Am I mistaken or will there be a full moon tonight?"

Brenda leaned across, "Perfect for skinny dipping with this heat!"

***

An hour later, Lionel drove the Ford down the dirt path to the pond. Oaks and maples lined the way, emphasizing the creeping darkness of the setting sun. Julianne exclaimed happily at each bump. She kept one hand on the ceiling and one hand on Lionel's thigh. "When I was a freshman, people talked about Little Spy Pond, but we never met anyone who had ever been there"

Lionel nodded, "It's always a friend of a friend, right? It's your lucky day to meet a friend's friend." His voice chattered over a series of road divots.

Beside the No Trespassing sign, the car skidded to a stop with Julianne in the perfect place to absorb the beauty of the setting. Perhaps thirty feet in diameter, a grassy knoll bordered the water with a green on blue which captured the last light of day. A wooden dock extended out from the shore.

When his companion inhaled deeply, Lionel said, "You should see it under a full moon."

Julianne stepped out and stood on the dock before he had even rounded the hood of the car. While she removed her outer layer of clothing, Lionel stopped to watch. When he finally tore his eyes away, he studied the sky and willed the moon to take its time rising.

"Aren't you going to strip?" called Julianne.

"You bet," agreed Lionel and ran down the dock shedding his shirt and shoes and socks. He pulled up beside her when he realized she held up her hand to silence him.

"Did you hear a noise?" Julianne had stopped undressing.

Lionel struck a brave pose. "Who goes there?" Then he said to her out of the side of his mouth, "It's probably a frog."

"Amphibians are marvelous," said Julianne. She almost entered the water, but another thought struck her. "What if it's the owner? What if he has a shotgun?"

"The owner doesn't care as long as we leave it the way we found it," reassured Lionel.

Julianne shrugged out of her remaining clothes and lowered herself into the water. Lionel dove in after her, but when he broke the surface she shushed him. "I heard it again. I'm serious. There's something in the water."

"Okay," said Lionel, "But it's been a really sweltering day. Let's stay in until we cool off. Then I'll drive you right back into town." He dogpaddled closer and gave her a little nuzzle.

"All right," she said with a sparkle, "then let's see if you can catch me."

Two laps around the pool and Lionel closed in as Julianne lagged. "Now I'm going to get you," he declared.

Julianne held up her hands, "I mean it. I really heard a sound." She headed for the nearest shore while Lionel called after her. The knoll proved slippery and the pond became inescapable as she slid back into the water. She turned to find

Lionel brushing up against her. She grabbed his probing hand and twisted him around. "What's that?"

Lionel turned and saw someone else in the pond with them. He stood large, shadowed, and perhaps wearing diving gear, though the pond barely reached seven feet.

"Is it the owner?" asked Julianne. "We didn't mean anything! We wanted to cool off!"

"I'm the owner," muttered Lionel.

"What?" Julianne turned on him. His manner caused her face to redden with embarrassment shading toward fear. No longer worried about the stranger across the pond, she struggled through the water toward the dock. She would never make it before the newly unveiled owner.

Occasionally it's your voice which goes first when the lunar cycle strikes, thought Lionel the Werewolf. If it did not, then he might point out how much he enjoyed a good chase. At least, he thought he did. His memory would be the other part of him which tended to disappear. He had become a college dropout because he could not tolerate the fear of exposure among so many peers.

Weird how the strange silhouette across the way looked familiar. No time for such distractions when he needed to pursue the enticing figure climbing onto the dock.

***

Yellow filled Lionel's field of vision until he realized his eyelids blocked his view of the world. When he opened them, white and then specks and then the sky after sunrise filled his eyesight. Splinters made his backside hurt. When he moved, the dock had already become too hot. His naked skin might be sunburned by now.

"Good, you are awake," came a voice from the pond.

Sitting up and sprouting sore spots on his skin, Lionel growled in the general direction of the intruder. He stopped at the sight of the head protruding from the water's surface. "Do I know you? You look like the Creature from the drive-in."

"I am not the one from the lagoon." His voice sounded like a combination of a killer whale and Desi Arnaz. His skin shone like a piranha, matching his threatening teeth.

Quickly, Lionel scanned his surroundings and then his own body. His tongue dug in his teeth. "Did you happen to see a college girl around here?"

"I'm curious," said the Creature who was not the Creature, "why do you tell them you are not the owner of this property?"

"It's a lot easier to lure them out to trespass than it is to ask them if they want to swim naked in my backyard," confessed Lionel, immediately regretting his candor. "You do look familiar." Lionel pushed himself upright. He had definitely not eaten last night because he felt dizzy. He gathered up his scattered clothes and headed for the hidden path which led to his house.

The Werewolf paused twice to check the thing in the pond had stayed there. He showered and put on fresh clothes. Going about in the house for breakfast, he paused before the group portrait over the mantelpiece in his living room. He opened the hall closet, dug around behind the coats, and pulled out two more paintings. Then he brewed an extra cup of coffee and brought two steaming mugs to the back porch.

"Do you drink coffee?" he asked the Fish Guy, now seated on his rocker.

"I'm a social drinker," came the answer and the Creature sipped.

"I have seen you before," confirmed Lionel. "You're not in Putterdam's painting with my father."

"True. Putterdam completed it from memory. I never had the privilege of meeting the artist. In fact, your grandfather died moments before we could have met."

"My Uncle Sterling left my father a Frederic Church painting in which the three of you are standing with my uncle by a river in New York. The landscape is very well done. Igor thought my father would appreciate a pleasant view of the outdoors."

"I remember when we posed for it," said the Creature. "Church always worried about appearances. He made two renderings, one close and the other far. He insisted Igor never transfer the paintings to anyone. They were to be destroyed upon your uncle's death."

"So, you are the infamous Gil?" asked Lionel.

"As you are the infamous Lionel number a dozen plus. Have you seen Igor recently?"

Lionel gathered the china and headed inside.

"You have not, because your Uncle Igor wrote me and asked if I would look in on you," called Gil. "He is worried since the pack ostracized you."

Lionel hurried into the kitchen, made a racket, and returned. "They insisted on their ways and I contended we change with the times."

"This had nothing to do with you dropping out of medical school?" Gil held devilishly still as he spoke. "Did they tell you there has always been a Lionel in the pack and Lionel has always been the doctor?"

"They call it a physicker." Lionel dropped onto his wooden bench and sighed with exasperation. "You sound like you're from the pack? Igor would have…"

"Your uncle wanted to make sure you did not do anything stupid. I would say he had a right to be concerned. Werewolves don't hunt in their own backyard. I understand such behavior went out of fashion with the wolf hunts in the Middle Ages."

Lionel nodded. "I'm not going back to medical school."

"You still have to make a living," said Gil, sounding avuncular, "even if you are merely keeping up appearances."

"I don't suppose you even bother to work looking like…?" said Lionel.

"Something the boat cat dragged in?" Gil dug a claw into the armrest.

Lionel stood, "Would you like to see the Church painting? Igor left a few things with my father. If you're going to see him soon, maybe you could take them?"

***

The noise in the Pittsburgh Civic Arena grew to an outrageous level.

Igor spoke and Gil shook his head. Igor turned to his other side and spoke again. Sterling shrugged. Igor motioned toward the end of their aisle and shoved Gil in that direction. The trio shuffled through annoyed youths bopping to *Time Is On My Side*. They moved slightly faster to the section exit and out into the arena thoroughfare,

Igor spoke and his companions held up their hands to stop. Then they cleared wads of cotton from their ears.

"Well?" said Gil.

"We should go," said Igor. "I only came for Tommy Shondell anyway. Him and *Under My Thumb*."

"I'm fine with leaving," shouted Sterling.

"We paid for the tickets," said Gil. "We should stay."

"I'm rich. We're all rich," said Igor.

"Speak for yourself," said Gil.

"Between the three of us, we can travel anywhere and see the Rolling Stones in concert, even London." Igor checked his watch. "Besides, we need to drive out to Monroeville if you're going to see what I've been talking about." He headed for the arena exit. "Do either of you remember where we parked?"

***

Circling through side streets well east of Pittsburgh, the three occupants of the Cadillac Coupe DeVille looked conspicuous with the convertible top down. Still, the locals had seen plenty of strangeness in recent weeks. The unusual head shapes barely registered.

"No one has seen Ruthven in over a century," stated Sterling. "Mira still mourns Vlad. However, grieving has replaced her desire for his return."

"I'm glad you have been able to maintain your relationship with her," commented Igor.

"If you could forgive me, then perhaps...," said Sterling.

"We buried our grudges years ago," declared Igor.

"Mira's brain works differently from ours," said Sterling. "Perhaps Farrah understands, but I do not."

"Women," agreed Gil.

"He means they are both of supernatural origin. The three of us are simply unusually long-lived," said Igor.

"Nevertheless...," stipulated Gil.

They drove in silence until Sterling announced they had to turn. He held the map. Gil insisted they had already been down this road twice. Igor pulled onto the side of the road.

While Igor and Sterling huddled over the map, Gil asked, "Doesn't Lionel live nearby? When did you last hear from him?"

"He's in Indiana," said Sterling.

"Hopefully, if he stays quiet for another few years, the pack will lose his scent," said Igor.

"It's quite a coup extracting a victim from such cultish roots," said Sterling.

"Tell me about it," agreed Gil. "You parked in front of a church and their potluck dinner is letting out."

They hurriedly settled on a route and set out again. When they finally arrived at the cemetery gates, chains held the entry closed. They debated climbing over, breaking through, or picking the lock. In the end, Gil noticed the fence ended about twenty feet on either side of the gates. They opted to drive over the grass because they wanted to hide the coupe.

Unfortunately, they did not make it out of sight before they observed movement. Igor shut down the car and they stepped out among the gravestones.

"Remember, we only want to observe," said Igor. "This is the fourth rising I have seen. The only other surviving assistant passed word to me she had heard about dangerous manifestations near Harrisburg."

"How is Frau Blücher?" asked Sterling. "It's been centuries."

"Not well. Even the most fastidious of us cannot be saved by dedication to self-maintenance." Igor stared at his hands, studies in replacement parts. "Anyway, I wanted both of you here. We need to do something, but we will probably require the others."

"I was happy in Baja," Gil whispered. "I don't hear from you, Igor, for two years. You said, 'Let's see the Rolling Stones. We need to make a little side trip, but it'll be fun.' This hasn't been fun."

"There goes another one," Sterling pointed. "You believe they are related to Ruthven?"

"I didn't say what you apparently heard," replied Igor. "Ruthven heard about them and he told Lionel- an older one- and Lionel told Farrah." He motioned for Sterling and Gil to follow him into a mausoleum. Once inside, they found places to sit. "Word of Gil reached her the same way."

Gil snapped his fingers, "It has a nice echo."

"Think about it this way," Igor pointed at Sterling. "You were purely the product of technology. Arguably, so was I since I used the knowledge shared with me by morally ambiguous scientists to maintain my own being. Mira is another thing altogether. She is the creation of something we don't under-stand and we call it the supernatural for this reason."

Gil raised a hand, "Do me."

"You and the werewolves and whatever else are products of evolution or weird biological experiments or both. This leaves Farrah, who is in between Mira and Sterling, created on Earth by people using supernatural technology. And these zombies are like Farrah in that regard."

"I doubt Farrah would be happy to hear you compare her to anyone else," said Gil.

Sterling sighed so heavily dust rose from the stone surfaces. "How could Ruthven be responsible for these monsters? He never made it this far north."

"I'm not saying he's responsible. We'll never know where they come from. The important thing is we stop them."

Gil shook his head. "You mention Ruthven one more time and I'm ready to go home." He slid upright.

"First they come for the zombies. Next they come for us," explained Igor. "How long will it take for humanity to finish off these walking dead things before they notice how many other unusual creatures have moved into their neighborhoods?"

"The zombies are killing people though, right?" argued Gil.

Igor and Sterling looked at him.

"Fine, I agree you have a point," said Gil. "Let's go out there and put them back in the ground."

"There is one problem. This is only one cemetery. Listen!" Igor shushed them. Many feet and moans could be heard out-side the crypt walls. "I find more and more of these creatures with each new eruption. We need to ask for help from Mira and Farrah, even Lionel, if we are going to put a stop to them."

***

Mira stepped through the broken glass of the Spencer Gifts shop onto the runway of the mall. She raised the head dangling from her left hand, "How is this thing still alive?" Indeed, the mouth on the decapitated head continued to chew on what appeared to be its own tongue. A moment later, the meat vanished down its throat only to drop with a splotch onto the disgusting tiled floor. Then, the face silently burped.

"You have a little something there," Sterling said from the cracked coin-operated horse. He pointed at his own chest.

Using her free hand, Mira tugged at her t-shirt, which said, "Are you ready to fire your works for the Bicentennial?!?" She scraped a little blood from the suggestive bottle rocket picture in the middle. "It's barely noticeable." She walked over to the fountain, now filled with a brown congealing mess, and plunged the head into it. After visibly counting to thirty, she extracted the head, "See, still not completely dead."

Sterling shrugged. He had already dismounted. He took the head and smashed it against the inside of the concrete fountain border, sending a spray of decayed, putrid head cheese into the rotten, fetid broth already contained in the pool "Not anymore now."

Mira slid an arm into Sterling's and they promenaded past empty jewelers, soundless record stores, and deserted arcades, disturbing the dust on every surface they touched. At the J.C. Penney, a head flew in their direction, rolling to a stop at their feet. The missing face and brains left the zombie fully departed.

Igor stepped out of the department store, pointed a thumb behind him, and announced, "All clear." He joined his two companions as they strolled.

"I understand Farrah is involved in a project down in Washington, but there must be someone who can help us," said Farrah.

"You've never met Gil, have you?" said Sterling.

"I'm not sure the two of you would enjoy one another's company," said Igor.

Mira asked, "Why?"

Igor and Sterling shared a look behind her back.

"Of course, we could invite young Lionel," suggested Igor.

Mira's knuckles paled even more than normal.

"You can't forget what his grandfather did," noted Sterling.

"He left the pack," said Igor after they had proceeded a little further through the wreckage of the abandoned mall. "He could use a new family. The old one is not exceedingly kind to those they deem beyond the pale."

Sterling added, "One might see befriending the current Lionel as the perfect vengeance on all those Lionels who came before..."

"Fine!" Mira's yell bounced through the great space. "I will see this new Lionel because he intrigues me. I make no promises, but you can bring him to my residence in the autumn. It will be enjoyable to watch the pup run in the moonlight."

"Thank you, Countess," said Igor.

Mira pulled away from the other two, "Are we finished here?"

"Not quite," answered Sterling. He extended his extensive arm and pointed toward the former Sears. He walked past the vampire and led them to a seated figure, stopping twenty feet from the obvious zombie.

"What is he doing?" wondered Mira.

The undead creature sat on the bench, watching the Sears entrance. Beside him, a shopping bag from Higbee's rested.

"I can only assume he has body parts in the bag to snack on later," said Igor.

Sterling shook his head, "He's waiting. Isn't it obvious?"

"He's a zombie, not a shopper," said Igor. "You're imparting your own qualities to him."

"Come to think of it," posited Mira, "are you any different from a zombie? Aren't you reanimated?"

"I am a simulacrum," declared Sterling. "Unless a transplanted heart is a zombie organ, the creature and I have nothing in common."

"Really? A simulacrum?" said Mira.

Sterling raised a hand for silence. Then he slowly stepped closer to the sitting dead.

The Zombie watched him approach. It actually looked fearful when Sterling reached ten feet.

"Hello," offered Sterling.

"I'm waiting for my wife," said the Zombie in a dry, guttural voice. Then he had a coughing fit.

Sterling looked toward Igor and Mira. He mouthed, "It talks?"

After a great heaving expectoration, the Zombie said, "Of course I talk." It's voice came slowly, like a spouse who had spent too long in the auto parts store while their partner debated which windshield wiper to buy.

"My name is Sterling."

"I'm Brian," said the Zombie. It's hand reached from the end of a rotted arm.

"You know you're dead?" yelled Mira.

Brian stood carefully and wobbled for a moment. He tested his legs and adjusted. This happened three times before he felt steady enough to turn around. He took in the rest of the mall. "What the hell happened here?" His voice did not vary in tone. He noted the Vampire and her companion. "What happened?"

"Sterling, deal with him and let's clear out the Sears so we can leave," insisted Mira.

"I'm going to wait here with Brian while you two tidy up the big store. Think you can handle it?" asked the Simulacrum.

Mira hated taking direction. She refused to look at Sterling or Brian as she led Igor past the map of the Sears interior.

Sterling gestured for Brian to retake his seat before joining him on the bench. "You've been here for over a week."

"I try not to hurry Marcia," said Brian.

"She's dead or worse," said Sterling.

A long minute passed.

"Am I dead?" asked Brian.

"We're a lot alike, Brian," said Sterling. "You'd be amazed what you can do with flesh and bone if you still have a mind."

"I really wish Marcia would come back. I feel like I haven't eaten in ages."

"My friend, Igor, is clever," said Sterling. "I bet we can put our heads together and figure out a way to take your mind off your hunger and see if you can be an actual living dead. Would you like that, Brian?"

Brian's cheek twitched with an attempted smile. His lip split revealing an exceptional amount of gum. "Beats the alternative."

ABOUT A ZOMBIE

On the West Coast Trail in British Columbia, Brian and Sterling walked alongside a majestic view. They had been at it for an hour.

"You say there are ladders and rope bridges on this hike?" commented Brian.

"Uh-huh," agreed Sterling.

Brian could not take his eyes off Sterling's huge feet. Even after all these decades, the old monster still wore boots which looked like three pairs of Doc Martins sewn together with barbell weights for soles.

The path behind them displayed regular indentations of two sets of massive hiking shoes. If they plummeted to their demise, at least they would be easy to track. Brian imagined being trapped for weeks in a crevasse with Sterling.

"You have taken this trail before?" asked Brian. When he decided to visit Sterling three months ago, Brian walked much of the way from Wyoming. Further hiking had not been on his agenda post-arrival. Sterling had complained they both looked too pale and the fresh air would do them good.

"Never," said Sterling.

Thirty minutes elapsed before they reached the base of the first ladder. They stood in silence and contemplated the climb.

"It would be a shame to ruin the trail for anyone who comes after us," said Brian.

"You are suggesting we turn back for the good of others?" asked Sterling.

Brian shrugged.

"Don't do that again," said Sterling urgently.

"Do what?"

"The shrugging," Sterling reached out and pressed the side of Brian's head above the left ear. "You've sprung a leak."

"Does it look bad?" asked the Zombie.

"Bad is relative for those like us," said Sterling before pulling his hand away. "A section of skull fell off you."

"Did you see where it landed?"

"Part of your brain is sticking to my hand," added Sterling.

"Sounds bad," said Brian, even as his enunciation wavered.

"Don't faint on me," said Sterling. "It's not a good look when I emerge into a clearing carrying an unconscious body. People talk. At times they talk about retrieving pitchforks."

"Rifles are worse," said Brian as he passed out.

***

Sterling the Simulacrum called Farrah the Mummy, who had an RV. Then he called Igor who had never been board certified in any medical specialty but had a wonderful laboratory in the basement of his current home in Montana. Farrah arrived after a thirty hour drive.

Sterling spent the time following Igor's care instructions delivered over frequent FaceTime calls. Igor spent an inordinate portion of their conversations reminding him whose idea it had been for them all to obtain iPhones and matching friends and family call plans. Igor used this as a counterweight to his insistence that all their ministrations were experiments since no one had ever researched keeping zombies alive.

Farrah and Sterling stretchered Brian into the bed at the back of the Winnebago. Sterling agreed Brian looked very pale. They faced an eighteen hour drive to Helena.

Once they crossed into Washington and the sun had set, Farrah asked, "Is he the last of his kind?" Unsure if Sterling heard her, she added, "Because I'm the last. You're sort of the only one. Didn't Igor say the other assistants are dying off?"

"There are always more vampires and werewolves," said Sterling.

"Gil is one of a kind even if there are other fish people."

"This is so," agreed Sterling.

"So, what about Brian?"

"If we learned the method, we could make another me or you or Igor or even Brian," said Sterling. He watched her steer down another mountain. "You ponder the ineffable."

"Not really. I ponder a world without zombies."

***

Farrah, Sterling, and Igor took turns ministering to Brian. He had begun to come apart. Igor tried to stop or at least inhibit the process. The former Mad Scientist Assistant had become an expert surgeon, biologist, and all the other -ist's over his years of self-preservation. Rotted flesh did not however respond to grafts and medicine like his own skin did. Personally, he could always step in before an organ reached a critical state, but Brian existed as a collection of past-due parts.

"Why do you always put your lab in the basement?" asked Sterling during one changing of the guard with Igor.

"I appreciate proximity to civilization," came the answer, "as opposed to the folks who build a shack in the middle of nowhere. Civilization however does not necessarily approve of my interests."

"I do walk into town occasionally," said Sterling.

"My compromise is being careful how much attention I can afford," said Igor. "Besides, my apprenticeships all involved dungeon work. In my day, no mad scientist worked above ground or during daylight hours. Times change. I've adapted."

Sterling stood very still until he looked Igor in the eye. "I have always appreciated your ability to change."

Left alone a moment later, Igor used a gore-soaked rag to wipe away a tear.

"Ding dong!" Came a shout from upstairs. Mira descended like a B movie queen aiming for her closeup. The pet carrier she held before her hindered the effect.

"What's all this?" asked Igor, wishing Farrah or Sterling had announced the Countess.

Mira disburdened herself on a nearby table and moved near to Brian. She studied him with obvious dismay. "He's quite a mess."

Discombobulated, Igor murmured, "One does one's best," before gathering himself, "Not everyone departs for the undiscovered country and then..." Igor stumbled for words.

"Lost your metaphor?" asked Mira.

Igor waved his hands in the air, "What did you bring?"

"We finally detained the horrible feline you infested my home with. We're now fighting a plague of zombie mice. Local pest control no longer accepts my calls. I thought the little beast might be useful. Maybe you could dissect it in lieu of our dear friend, but I appear to be too late."

"When did you become so fabulous?" asked Igor.

"This existence is long. Personalities are few." Mira pursed her lips before ejaculating, "Gotta try them all."

"Are you stalking Pokémon Go gamers now?" asked Igor.

"Vampirism doesn't work that way, which you know."

Igor returned to Brian's bedside. "Most of what you see is Brian's inability to keep himself together." Igor side-eyed the Vampire. "You could suck his desiccated blood. Or nibble on it."

Mira threw herself into the only comfortable chair nearby. She wiggled into an indentation clearly left by Sterling. "When I last saw you, I thought you might be on the edge of surrendering to oblivion. Are we now laughing in the face of death?"

Fighting his way through a fog of confusion brought by her sudden treatment of him as worthy of emotional attention, Igor turned slowly, "You want to talk to me?"

"I came all this way. I brought your pet back. Brian is pretty much dead to the world. So, yes, I'm talking to you."

Igor organized his tools on their tray before speaking, "When I stopped believing the master knew best, I found a lifetime of philosophy draining away, leaving me empty and free. Instead, I consumed experiences and knowledge, filling the emptiness. All emotions are not created equal."

"Including sulking around a basement," interrupted Mira. "Now you're on the humor stage. Good for you. What about Brian? I was there when Sterling and you adopted him."

"You hardly describe..."

"It works well enough." Mira rose and headed for the stairs. "Fix him. I can't explain it, but I'd prefer a world with all of you in it."

Igor watched her disappear up the steps. Then he turned to the pet carrier and extracted the cat. One eyeball swung loosely. When he gripped the animal's midsection, his thumb sunk between bones, scraping dried flesh and something moist which might be the remains of a recently devoured mouse brain. "Did sweetums miss your papa?"

In gratitude for the freedom, the cat dragged a chipped claw down Igor's forearm and leapt for the darkness. After pursuing the fleet-footed fiend around the basement, Igor gave up when it slipped behind the water boiler. He needed to tend the dreadful gash.

***

At breakfast the next morning, Sterling announced he would catch a ride with Mira when she left. He then polished off the last box of oatmeal in the house.

In a quiet moment, Mira asked Igor for a shopping list, making it sound like she would resupply him before departing. She then asked for directions to a place for food. Also, money. Also, instructions for the purchasing of goods.

By this point, Sterling had overheard enough and offered to take Mira to the supermarket. They needed directions and cash. Then the obvious problem hit them. Mira could not go outside, or near any window. She offered to stay with Brian while the other two did the necessary.

Cycling between the basement and the first floor, Mira kept her ear peeled for the return of her friends. While near the Zombie, she maintained a monologue about the importance of letting go. When on her own, she paged through Igor's books on medical science.

By the time Igor's Subaru pulled into the garage, Mira had grown irritably depressed. While the Simulacrum and the Well-Patched Man put away the groceries, Mira dropped a textbook on the counter and announced, "Humans are too fragile to live! Have you actually looked at any of these books? Why do they even bother?"

Igor wiped off a juice carton. "Says the person who can be destroyed by spice and crossed sticks."

Sterling laughed, "Or a really big splinter."

Mira slammed the tome shut. "I am nigh invincible to time. They all rot away, not unlike poor Brian."

Igor went to her and she backed away out of fear he might hug her, but he stopped a yard away. Then he rolled up his sleeve. "See the stitch work? That's a repair. Homo sapiens can be repaired when they suffer an injury. All those books of mine which you have pulled from my shelves and not put back- they explain how amazing human biology can be."

Mira opened a drawer and took out a small, sharp knife. She dragged it down her own forearm. "Now how about I do it to you, Igor?" By the time she finished the question, her wound had closed.

"I'd rather not spend the time sewing right now. The ice cream will melt."

While Igor had his back to her, Mira asked, "Do you ever miss the time you spent in service to the Count and me?"

Igor froze before the refrigerator.

Sterling stepped between the two of them. "Mira, the sun should be setting soon. How about offering me a ride home?"

Igor spoke into the open freezer, "I will be fine with Brian. I have your numbers if I need to reach you."

***

Igor lifted his head and peeled the scalpel from his cheek, where it had adhered with his drool. He had fallen asleep next to Brian's *corpus deficiens*. Alone with the fading zombie for four days, Igor had tried most insane ideas.

Today he planned his last desperate attempt, revived from long ago. He had spent the pre-dawn hours stealing car batteries from a dealership on the other side of town.

"It's just as well Sterling is not here," muttered Igor through mucky, exhausted lips. "Though there is no earthly reason a powerful electric shock should revive a zombie. His heart has not beat for decades. But still... the brain of a zombie might be the key. It's electrical synapses are the most likely repository of the self-ness which grants all monsters their personhood, whether natural or supernatural."

Igor pushed himself up and went to his phone and recorded the entire prior speech. He might need the words for the science paper he planned to publish when all of this finished. He would choose one of the online journals and bypass a peer review.

Later, jumper cables attached, arcane wiring stretched to the thirty amp outlet, and poised beside a recently installed oversized electrical throw switch, Igor sent enough current through Brian to stagger a selection of dogs in the toy category.

Surprisingly, Brian's eyes shifted from side to side.

Tilting his head back for a preternatural outcry, Igor shouted, "He's a-...!"

Brian's harsh voice exhaled, "Igor? Please don't... raise your voice."

Not for the first time, Igor swallowed his words. Also, not for the first time, he wondered how zombies produce any vocal sound.

The moment of joy quickly passed. Igor brought Brian smoothies of organs from his personal stores. Brian's brain may have resumed its function, but the body remained a disaster. He could manage a few feet with a walker though he spent most of his time in the living room on the recliner. Whether a nerve cell slurry or a jellied hemisphere, food dropped through his torso at an alarming rate.

"How have you managed to wear any pants?" inquired Igor.

"Depends," answered the Zombie.

"On what?"

Unlike a living person, Brian barely dozed. Unfortunately, he had limited tolerance for television. "Igor!"

Not gifted with whatever passed for zombie metabolism, Igor required rest. He did not receive nearly enough over the next three weeks. Igor found messages from Mira, Sterling, Gil, Farrah, and Lionel, but he did not have the energy to call back. His days passed in a blind stumbling of task after task all enforced by the necessities of continued living for his houseguest and himself.

Igor considered poisoning Brian, but he could not find the time to create an adequate formula. He carried an icepick in his back pocket for two days before he noticed a strip of muscle dangling from Brian's left calf. Igor found comfort in the likelihood he would outlast the shedding dead.

***

Igor returned to himself and found he stood before the blender. He poured the pureed brain into a cup and considered washing the pitcher. With a shrug he decided nothing growing in it would harm Brian and returned it to the blender base.

His next moment of awareness arrived and Igor stood in the kitchen doorway holding the glass in one hand and a straw in the other. Brian could not use a straw, so Igor studied the contents of both his hands and wondered what had occurred during the previous few minutes. The strobe light illuminating his life spent more time on darkness.

He watched Brian as the Zombie stared at the big screen television.

The doorbell rang.

Experiencing a rush of fear, he carried the brain shake to Brian. He looked to see what Brian watched. The nature documentary followed a pack of hyenas.

The chimes sounded again and Igor thought about chimes at midnight and the bell tolling for someone and so many other references dredged by his own brain which had become a slurry of exhaustion.

"What fresh horror is this?" said Igor. The ice pick sat on the bookshelf beside the TV. Igor retrieved the implement of zombie destruction.

"Hello!" called Sterling from inside the house. "We thought you might have your hands full and let ourselves in."

Sterling and Farrah filled the entryway until Mira and Lionel pushed their way to the front. Then Gil's face appeared behind everyone. They waved to Brian.

Igor slid the weapon behind his back. He mumbled a greeting and sidestepped into the kitchen. The sounds from the other room told him the rest had gathered around the debilitated Zombie. They sounded cheerful, which was an unusual song for anyone in the group, let alone as a unison chorus.

Gil joined Igor, "Brian looks worse than I imagined. Even Romero wouldn't cast him. You should have gone ahead and used the icepick."

Mira walked in and nodded her agreement.

Lionel wiped aside tears, "Sterling is sitting with him. They're reminiscing. I need a drink."

Igor looked at the icepick in his hand and dropped it into the sink. "I found a way to bring him back after you left," he said to Mira. "Did I do the right thing?"

A dark and frightening gloom crossed Mira's face before she went to the basement door and descended.

At the next opportune moment, Igor slipped downstairs after her. She sat in the recliner, seemingly asleep. "You don't need to be quiet. I'm resting my eyes. Did you come down here for my blessing to end the zombie?"

"I want to do whatever I can for him." Igor turned his head side to side, releasing a hideous crack. "Have you ever seen the musical *Cats*?"

"You go to the theater?" said Mira.

"Did you know it's based on a book of poetry?"

"You read poetry?"

Igor ignored the mocking Vampire. "The musical centers on the cats wanting to be chosen for a journey to the Heaviside Layer, a stand-in for heaven. The thing is the poems never mention any such place. It was added to help the story make sense."

Mira pulled the lever on the chair and rapidly sat upright. "I noticed the strangest thing when I spent time with you and Farrah and Sterling centuries ago. I lost my taste for killing. Not for blood- which I retain because I will surely end when that happens. I developed a tenderness for my food. Before, I toyed with young men for hours before ripping open their throats. I do not ache with guilt. I am fundamentally different now."

"Are you saying I have gone soft?" asked Igor.

"No," answered Mira, "I'm asking how you are different than the you from earlier days. I once told you it can be an exceedingly long life. Parts of us are eternal, while other aspects are mutable. The Igor I knew would never lose his ability to dispose of an inconvenient scientific subject. I respected your decisiveness." She rose to her feet. "Be the Igor whom Brian requires, not the one who skulked in shadows, fearful of his master."

Sitting alone, Igor fingered the nearby instrument tray. He sought answers even as he heard his cat approach. The creepy feline moved in a weird march as she threw paws forward in a dangle of sinews and dislocated bones. Still, the beast held Igor's attention as it nuzzled his shelf of exotic glassware.

***

Dinner proved unmemorable. Each houseguest excused himself. Igor finally followed Farrah into the family room and watched her sit beside Brian, sharing a few quiet words. Unusually, Lionel and Gil cleaned up after the meal. Left with nothing to do, Igor stayed with the rest until Sterling lifted Brian.

Mira held the basement door while the Simulacrum headed down the steps.

At a loss, Igor followed.

Sterling placed the Zombie on the bed. He turned and faced Igor. The Monster's face had gone from gray to light blue. "The three of us discovered Brian. We're as close to family as he has." Then words failed Sterling.

Mira coughed. "Sterling has offered to end Brian's existence. He will destroy the brain and we can all move on."

Igor looked back and forth. "I'll do it."

Sterling silenced Mira before she could object. He nodded and led her upstairs.

An hour later, Igor joined everyone upstairs. Being Monsters, none of them shed tears. It took a few hours to dispose of the zombie remains, even with everyone chipping in.

***

Two days later, Igor said goodbye to Lionel who had lingered because his flight had been delayed. After a nap, the scientist in him could wait no longer and headed downstairs. As he opened the locked cabinet in the darkest corner, his pet cat brought him a mouse and dropped it at his feet.

Igor thanked the feline, "You remember our friend, Brian," he said as he extracted a brain in a jar from a shelf. Stray cells had flaked off the cerebral matter and shifted loosely in the fluid. Igor carried the floating organ to his work table. "What am I going to do with you, old friend?"

LONE
WOLF
THE MONSTERS
WILL RETURN!

ALSO BY KOJ BOOKS

Five Raging Hearts: Splatterpunk for the Soul

Three novellas and two short stories from the hearts of Craig Brownlie, Roxane Llanque, Mathew L. Reyes, Judith Sonnet, and Wile E. Young, with an introduction by Bitter Karella

<u>Read all the Little Books of Pain:</u>
#1 Hammer Nail Foot
#2 Thick As A Brick
#3 A Book Of Practical Monsters

<u>For YA, MG, and Young at Heart readers:</u>
Comic Book Summer

About the Author

Abbott and Costello starred in the movies which introduced Craig to monsters. By the time he saw Steve McQueen in *The Blob*, Craig could just about cope. This was in broad daylight on weekend afternoons in the safety of his parents' home. Also, the television screen was really small. None of this stopped him from checking out all the Alfred Hitchcock anthologies from the library- think classic horror mixed with R.L. Stine.

Look for his work in Space and Time Magazine, *Demons and Death Drops*, *No More Resolutions*, *Lovecraftiana*, and *Unspeakable Horrors 3*. He contributes randomly to Uncomfortably Dark.

Visit Craig and sign up for his newsletter at
https://craigbrownlie.com/
Friend him on Facebook. Follow him on Twitter/X and Instagram. Or talk to him at a convention.